DO NOT REMOVE
CARDS FROM POCKET

Beyond the Labyrinth

 A Richard Jackson Book

BEYOND THE
LABYRINTH

Gillian Rubinstein

ORCHARD BOOKS   NEW YORK

This work was assisted by a writer's fellowship from the Australia Council, the Federal Government's arts funding and advisory body.
Creative Writing programme assisted by the Literature Board of the Australia Council, the Federal Government's arts funding and advisory body.

The quotation on the frontispiece is taken from *Klingsor's Last Summer* and used with kind permission of the trustees of the estate of Hermann Hesse. Translation copyright © 1970 by Farrar, Straus and Giroux, Inc. Reprinted by permission of Farrar, Straus and Giroux, Inc. Quotations from *Monty Python and the Holy Grail* are used with kind permission of Python (Monty) Pictures Ltd. Quotations from *Notes on the Narangga Tribe of the Yorke Peninsula* are used with kind permission of the author, D.L. Hill.

Orchard Books, A division of Franklin Watts, Inc.
387 Park Avenue South, New York, NY 10016

Manufactured in the United States of America.
Book design by Mina Greenstein.
The text of this book is set in 11 pt. Electra.
10 9 8 7 6 5 4 3 2 1

Library of Congress Cataloging-in-Publication Data
Rubinstein, Gillian. Beyond the labyrinth / by Gillian Rubinstein.
— 1st American ed.   p.   cm. "Originally published in Australia"—T.p. verso.
"A Richard Jackson book"—Half t.p.
Summary: Fourteen-year-old Brenton questions the choices in his life when an alien anthropologist arrives to study an ancient Aboriginal tribe that once lived in the area around his home.
ISBN 0-531-05899-9.   ISBN 0-531-08499-X (lib. bdg.)
[1. Extraterrestrial beings—Fiction.   2. Science
Fiction.   3. Australia—Fiction.]   I. Title.
PZ7.R83133Be 1990 [Fic]—dc20 90-30627 CIP AC

For my sister, Jocelyn,
who knows the more excellent way

But even children, though they
are far ahead of adults in cleverness,
are perplexed and alone when they
confront fate.

HERMANN HESSE: *A Child's Heart*

Contents

THE WAY IN

1

NORMALLY his name is Brenton Trethewan and he is fourteen years old, but right now he is a nameless and ageless hero, involved in a dangerous, deadly quest. His thin, rather small body is lying on the rug of his bedroom floor, but his mind is away in the *Labyrinth of Dead Ends*, where he's trying to decide if he should stand and fight the Trollwife of the Cave or if he should leap up and grasp the iron chain that swings over his head. At the moment he's high on skill, low on stamina and low on luck, and he lost his shield two moves before.

He throws the dice thinking, If the score's higher than six I'll fight, and if it's lower I'll go for the chain. He's faced the Trollwife before and he's never got past her.

Three and two fall uppermost.

"Turn to page 115," the book tells him. He turns the pages hurriedly and reads:

> The iron chain is a booby trap. As you grasp it the roof of the tunnel you are in collapses and you are buried alive under tons of rock. Your part in this adventure is over.

"Aw!" Brenton exclaims. He pushes the book away, scoops up the dice and rolls over onto his back. He is lying there, wondering whether to resurrect himself from beneath 3 the tons of rock and set out again through the *Labyrinth of Dead Ends,* when the door of his bedroom flies open and a pile of bedclothes walks in. Somewhere underneath it is his brother, Michael.

"What the hell do you think you're doing, Mick?" Brenton demands. There's no answer from the animated pile of bedclothes; it staggers across the room, kicks aside the *Labyrinth of Dead Ends* and collapses in a heap against the wall under the window. From beneath it Michael Trethewan emerges. A look of amusement mixed with trepidation crosses his face as he foresees the devastating effect his words are going to have on his older brother.

"Mum says I've got to move in with you!"

"What!" Brenton shrieks in horror.

Chris Trethewan appears at the door. "Vicky's going to have Mick's room and Mick's going to share with you." When Brenton groans in disbelief she goes on angrily, "Brenton I *told* you that."

"You can't have told me loud enough. I must have been blocking it out. I probably didn't believe anything so terrible could actually happen." He is up off the floor now and retreating toward his bed. "Why can't Vicky share with Shelley? That makes much more sense!"

"No it doesn't," his mother retorts. "Shelley needs a room of her own—she's nearly seventeen and Vicky's only twelve. Now take this end of Michael's bed and help me lift it in."

"It's much worse for me," Michael observes gloomily, looking around the room. "Imagine trying to go to sleep with World War III all over the walls."

"Brenton can take all that down," his mother says rather breathlessly, struggling with the bed.

"No, Brenton cannot!" he returns promptly, letting his end of the bed down with a thud on the floor. He looks

4

possessively at his nuclear weapons collection. The entire wall above his bed is covered with pictures of mushroom clouds, nuclear explosions and weapons, newspaper articles and statistics, from Hiroshima to Star Wars. Framed in black a picture of a clock shows the hands at three minutes to midnight.

"They give me nightmares," Michael complains.

"I'm not surprised," Chris agrees, looking at the collection distastefully and frowning. "They'd give me nightmares too."

"It's not the stuff on the walls that gives me nightmares," Brenton says. "They're just pictures. What gives me nightmares are the things themselves. Taking the pictures down isn't going to get rid of them." His voice is faintly accusing and he looks defiantly at his mother as though he holds her personally responsible for the nonpeaceful use of atomic fission.

"At least we wouldn't have to think about them all the time," she says.

"You should be thinking about them all the time," he returns seriously. His mother gives him a helpless look and changes the subject.

"Help Mick with his bed and then come and do the washing up. And, Mick, you'd better have some breakfast. We must get the house straight before I leave for the airport."

When she is no longer in the room Brenton confides in Michael, "I can't stop thinking about them."

"I know," Michael says awkwardly.

It is typical of Brenton that he should switch from open hostility to vulnerability in a few seconds. Michael looks at him with reluctant compassion and then shrugs his shoulders. Lately he has been starting to see Brenton no longer as the older brother who has always been an inseparable **5** part of his life, but as a quite distinct and different person, a person who often puzzles and irritates him, but who in some curious way needs his understanding and even his protection. Michael is already, at twelve, taller than his brother. He is heavily built with blue eyes and sandy hair, while Brenton has inherited the dark coloring and slight build of some remote Cornish ancestor, along with other traits that make him both stubborn and dreamy. Michael is not only physically the stronger of the two, emotionally and mentally he is more robust.

He feels sorry for Brenton, but as usual he is unable to give the help he dimly realizes Brenton needs. It makes him want to get away. Being with Brenton is too disturbing, too painful.

The moment extends itself unbearably. Finally Michael mumbles, without looking at his brother, "Think about something else. That's what I do."

"Yeah," Brenton attacks scornfully, aware that he has let down his defenses and needs to build them up again rapidly. "Fishing, sailing and cricket! You won't be able to do them in the nuclear winter!"

"I might as well enjoy them now then," Michael replies equably. He picks up the pile of bedclothes and slings it haphazardly on his bed. Anyone who has been out fishing on the gulf since four in the morning, as he has, finds it hard to believe in the nuclear winter. The idea of breakfast is a lot more real.

2 "YOU'RE NOT expecting me to look after her?" Mick stops eating toast and jam long enough to stare at his mother in outrage.

"You used to think she was OK," Brenton says. He is washing the breakfast dishes in a desultory fashion, staring out of the window and wondering if the faint lavender-colored haze between sky and sea could be the result of French nuclear tests in the Pacific.

"I did not! Anyway that was eons ago." Even as Michael speaks a faint memory does return to him and he wrinkles up his nose as if he can smell smoke. He gets up from the table to put two more slices of bread in the toaster. It doesn't want to go down. He thumps it hard.

"Mick," his mother remonstrates. "You've got to treat it gently. And if you finish the bread now you'll have to eat homemade for lunch. I'm not buying a loaf of shop bread every day just for you."

"Aw, Mum," he replies as the toaster finally surrenders and receives the white slices into itself. "You can't toast homemade bread. It clogs up the toaster. Besides, shop bread tastes better."

"There speaks your genuine little Aussie," Brenton comments sarcastically. "White bread, tomato sauce and candy! Building a nation of heroes!"

"It's building this hero without any problems," Michael says complacently, spreading the white toast with butter and jam. "You're just jealous because you've stopped growing." He regards his brother critically as he sinks his teeth into the toast. "It's not my fault you're a dwarf." 7

Brenton makes no response to this gibe, but the rate at which Michael has overtaken him is something that bothers him. I must be stunted, he thinks as he gazes out of the window toward the horizon. I've been adversely affected by invisible radiation. I'm a mutant. I'll be small forever. He has an unpleasant vision of his younger brother towering over him. He peers up at him like Jack the Giant Killer. I'll jump on his toes, he thinks madly. Bite him on the kneecap, fart in his general direction. . . .

"Hurry up, Brenton!" Shelley Trethewan is waiting impatiently, towel in hand, drying the cutlery and dishes as soon as Brenton puts them in the rack. "Mum, he's so slow," she complains. "I want to go down to the beach."

Brenton moves even more slowly. He takes a knife from the drain board and washes it with meticulous care as if it were a rare treasure. Just as he is placing it with painstaking precision in exactly the right spot on the rack, a car pulls up in the yard outside. A horn toots entreatingly.

"That's Jason," Shelley exclaims, a happy smile spreading over her broad, freckled face. With sandy hair the same color as Michael's, she is an attractive girl with large laughing eyes and a tall, slim figure. She drapes the towel around Brenton's neck. "Gotta dash," she says. "Can't keep the lad waiting. You'll have to finish it off!"

"Shelley!" Brenton yells in rage, tearing the damp towel off and throwing it ineffectually after her, but she is already in the front seat of the old brown Valiant; she cannot hear him. The Valiant pulls away with a shriek of rubber and a cloud of dust. Brenton appeals to his mother. "It's not fair! She never does her share!"

"You could wash a bit faster, Brenton. You were infuriating her, you know."

8   "Don't you want me to do it properly?" he retorts.

Chris sighs. It's the first day of the Australian summer holidays, and she foresees arguments over the washing up stretching ahead till February. Trying to be fair she says, "Mick, you help Brenton, please, when you've finished eating."

"Yeah," Brenton chips in. "How come you're still guzzling? I finished breakfast hours ago."

"Ah, but you weren't out fishing at four o'clock, were you?" Mick pours himself a cup of tea from the pot on the table. He adds sugar and milk and takes a tentative sip.

"This tea's cold!" he says in surprise.

"What the hell do you expect?" Brenton inquires. "It's been sitting on the table for an hour."

"Brenton!" his mother warns. It's not the swearing she objects to so much as the aggressive tone of voice. Brenton doesn't reply. He looks out of the window at the haze. He washes another knife. Michael drinks his cold tea.

"What did you get?" his mother asks.

"Not much. A few Tommies and four squid. I put the Tommies in the freezer. I'll take the squid up to the hotel later and see if they'll buy them."

Brenton has put two plates in the rack. Now he balances a saucepan upside down between them. He puts a cup on top of the saucepan. The saucepan wobbles. The cup slides off it onto the floor and smashes.

"Brenton!" Chris exclaims angrily.

"I can't help it," he explains. "No one's drying the things up, so there's no room for them in the rack."

"Michael, please stop eating and do the drying up *now*."

"It's not my turn to dry," Michael replies. "I don't mind washing. Brenton can dry." He gets up from the table and brings his plate and cup over to the sink.

"Brenton, let Michael finish the washing, and you do

the drying, *please*." Chris's voice is muffled as she reaches into the cupboard below the sink for a dustpan and brush.

"I've nearly finished the washing," Brenton points out.

Michael puts his plate and cup down and leans slowly and deliberately against his brother. Brenton pushes back with all his strength. For about thirty seconds they strive silently by the sink, then Brenton's foot slips in a damp patch left by the falling cup. He falls sideways, knocking the dustpan out of his mother's hand and hitting his shoulder on the wall. Michael begins to wash with silent efficiency.

Chris gives Brenton's leg, which is lying in front of her, a swift, sharp slap.

"Stop fooling around and get the drying done!" she shouts.

Brenton stares at her without moving. His face is closed, but calm as though he has just won a moral victory. "Now hit Mick," he tells her. "He started it."

Chris sweeps up the pieces of cup again, wraps them in newspaper and puts them in the bin. Then she speaks slowly and carefully.

"Brenton, Victoria is arriving here today to spend the next few weeks with us. I'll have to leave for the airport in an hour. I would like the washing up to be finished before that. Do you think that is possible?"

He gets up from the floor, shrugging. "I expect so," he says. He picks up the towel and starts drying the dishes.

"Weird name, isn't it?" Michael remarks cheerfully. "*Victoria!* A state. Imagine being called Tasmania!"

"Or New South Wales!" Brenton says. Both boys begin to laugh.

"Howya doing, Northern Territory?"

"Good to see ya, Queensland!"

Chris does not think they are very funny. "She's usually **10** called Vicky," she says rather coldly.

"Vicky and Micky," Brenton says, laughing even more. "Two dear little bunnies together, Vicky and Micky!"

Michael takes a swipe at him. Brenton parries it, karate style, and returns a snap kick. They have a brief and noisy spar.

"Watch out, Mick!" their mother says as he gets his foot caught behind the broom with which she is trying to sweep the kitchen floor. She puts her arm around him to restrain him and gives him a mock-ferocious shake. "Are you coming to the airport with me?"

"No way!" Michael says, disentangling himself and directing a punch and a final *hai* at Brenton. "I've got to sell my squid and then I'm going over to Danny's."

"Then you'll have to come, Brenton."

3 BRENTON groans, but he can't immediately think of any brilliant reason why he shouldn't go. It is always like this. Shelley and Michael *do* things; they have interests and hobbies and friends to share them with. The things they do are generally smiled on by their parents. Shelley plays tennis and squash. She takes the games seriously and plays them well. Michael plays cricket and is passionate about sailing and fishing. But Brenton is bored by sports, and sailing makes him seasick. He likes swimming, but he doesn't like being organized about it. He doesn't like being organized about anything. Most of all he likes just mucking around and fiddling with things. Possibly he has a brilliant and original mind, but no one has ever recognized it, partly because no one has ever been looking for it. Brenton himself does not recognize *11* it. He pretends not to be clever, because he learned at an early age that to be clever was to stand out in some way that was not appreciated by either children or parents. But even when he tries to do the same things as other people, he does them in a different way. He makes people uneasy.

His mother is watching him uneasily now. The drying up is finished. The breakfast dishes are cleared away. Brenton has carefully spread the towel on the rail to dry. Now he takes a pair of dice out of his pocket and throws them lightly from hand to hand. He frowns and whistles almost silently. He throws the dice casually onto the kitchen table, looks at the numbers and scoops them up again. He looks around at his mother and gives her a bafflingly cheerful smile.

"What time are we leaving?" he asks.

4 AS THE Falcon pulls out of the driveway and onto the road that will take them up the coast to the city, Chris Trethewan says anxiously to her son, "You will be nice to her, won't you?"

"I don't know yet," Brenton replies honestly. He thinks, Whatever the dice tell me: over six, I'll like her; six and under, I won't.

It's a game he has taken to playing lately. It amuses him to base decisions on chance. It seems to him a good approximation of what the universe is like—quite unpredictable and arbitrary. And it astonishes him that no one in his family has caught on to what he is doing.

Yesterday, playing cards with Michael, Brenton had secretly thrown the dice and the dice had told him to lose. He smiles now as he recalls the perverse feeling of power it gave him.

5 "YOU WANNA *play a game, Shell?"*
Michael shouts to his sister.

"What're you playing?" Shelley appears at the door of the family room, brushing her hair.

"Pandemonium. I won the last four games," Michael boasts.

"You beat Brenton four times in a row? I don't believe it!" She gives him a suspicious look. "Are you letting him win, Brenton?"

Brenton grins his maddening, secretive grin and says nothing. He shuffles a pack of cards with a snap, cuts it and pushes it across to Michael.

"Are you?" Michael demands, a look of dismay crossing his face as the joy of victory suddenly wanes.

"Why not?" Brenton asks. "You play to win, and you win. I play to lose and I lose. That way both of us win, and we're both happy."

But for Michael the essence of winning is that someone else should be beaten. "You idiot!" he yells, picking up the pack of cards and throwing it at his brother. "I'm going to start playing tricks on you!"

6 "WHY'S SHE got to come to us anyway?" Brenton asks his mother, his thoughts returning to Victoria.

"You know the whole family went to Africa a couple of years ago? Well, now Vicky's twelve she needs to go to a proper school, so she's going to boarding school in the city and coming to us for the holidays." Chris's expression is not happy as she tells Brenton this. In fact she is wishing she had never agreed to have Victoria. If she could go back to the moment when she made the decision she would revoke it.

7 GEOFF TRETHEWAN *guns his Commodore up the drive and slams the brakes on at the last moment. It's the way he always arrives home. It never fails to terrify Chris. She's afraid one day he will misjudge it, roll the vehicle or hit one of the children or animals that are always around the place.*

The door slams as he jumps out of the car, and the screen door slams too as he comes into the kitchen. He is a big man, sandy-haired like two of his children and blue-eyed. Dominating, energetic and forceful, he carries an air of possible violence about with him, which means he almost always gets

14 *his own way.*

He puts his arms around his wife and kisses her. She does not return his hug, but that may simply be because she is cooking dinner and her hands are floury.

"How was your day?" she asks.

"Bloody terrible. They're sounding me out again about shifting up north. Someone somewhere is trying to get rid of me. Bastards," he adds as an afterthought. "I've just got the new building completed too. No one else could have done it in that time within the budget. And once I'm out of the way, they'll try and close the hospital down."

"We can't leave here," Chris says anxiously. "This is our home. There's no way I'm going up north."

Geoff contemplates the future gloomily for a minute or two, then his natural high spirits reassert themselves. He gives his wife a pat on the rear. "We'll cross that bridge when we come to it. Any letters?"

"There's one over there from the Hares."

"They all still alive?"

"Very much so. Jenny says they're just starting to make headway; they're planning on staying indefinitely, and they want us to have Vicky."

"What, living here?"

"Just for the holidays. She'll be at boarding school most of the time."

"She's a bit young, isn't she?"

"She'll be twelve when she gets here. What do you think?"

Geoff is pouring himself a beer. "Get you a drink, love?"

"Yes, thanks, dear. Well?"

"Typical of Peter," Geoff observes, sucking deeply at the beer. "He's so keen to do good he expects someone else to look after his own kids."

"It's only Vicky."

"It's only Vicky now, but what happens when Simon needs   **15** *to go to school? I suppose we'll be asked to have him too. Can't they find anyone else? Why does it have to be us?"*

"I'm one of Jenny's oldest friends after all. We did our training together at the children's hospital. And they haven't any family in Australia. Peter came out from England and Jenny's parents are dead."

"What about what it costs?" Geoff complains. "We're finding it hard enough to get by—there's what we owe the bank on this place, and our own kids cost me an arm and a leg every time they get out of bed. It's not as though we've got two incomes," he adds, giving her a loaded glance.

"They're going to send money for her keep," Chris says, ignoring the implications of his last remark. "I think it would be good to have her; she's always been a lovely kid."

"I suppose it's up to you. You're the one that'll have to do the extra running around."

"I'm hoping Vicky will be quite a help in the house."

"OK then." He grins at her, puts down the empty glass, smacks his lips in satisfaction and gets another can from the fridge. "It's settled. When's she coming?"

"She starts school in February. I think I'll suggest to Jenny that she come at the beginning of the holidays. That way she can settle in before she goes away to school."

 "DON'T you want her to come?" Brenton asks astutely.

"Of course I do," Chris replies, putting aside her doubts. "I just hope you and Mick will make her feel at home."

"She used to be Mick's friend more than mine." Brenton

is trying to remember what she looks like, but his memories of her are fairly vague, even though their two families have been friends since before either of them was born. The motion of the car has put his mind into neutral, and suddenly there floats up to the surface of his memory a scene from years ago that he had completely forgotten until this moment.

9 "SAY YOU'RE SORRY!"

Michael is gasping as he surfaces. Brenton relentlessly pushes him underwater again. The sandy head bobs up spluttering, "Let go, Brenton, I'm drowning. Hel—!" He swallows a gulp of salty water as his head is pushed under again.

"Ouch!" Brenton lets go with a yelp as a small, wiry figure hurls itself onto him and bites one of the hands that are holding Michael down.

"You little monster!" Brenton says to Victoria in astonishment.

She is frantic with rage. "Leave him alone, you big bully!"

"He put a dead fish in my bed!"

"Serves you right!"

"I suppose you did it too." He grabs her by the wrists and holds her firmly. "You can apologize as well."

Victoria tries to kick him underwater, loses her balance and submerges. Michael, having recovered his breath, launches an attack on Brenton from behind. All three children disappear. When they surface Victoria and Michael are meters away, making swiftly for the shore. Brenton pursues **17** *them, arms flailing. He is the fastest swimmer, but they have a head start. By the time he reaches the shore they have all but vanished. He just sees a flicker of movement at the mouth of one of the caves. Stealthily he creeps up to the entrance and positions himself where he can jump on them if they come out. He feels like a hunter waiting patiently for his prey. "Vicky and Micky," he whispers to himself, "I'm going to get you!"*

10

"IS SHE coming all that way by herself?" he asks, half-enviously.

"Some friends of her parents are seeing her as far as Rome, and then she's coming on alone on the Qantas flight. The stewardesses look after unaccompanied children; she's probably having a marvelous time." Chris is driving fast now, holding the wheel lightly with one hand, her other arm leaning casually on the open window. The breeze is making her hair fly about.

Brenton is trying to picture someone leaving her family behind and taking off for a completely new life. Starting afresh. He wishes he could. He looks at his mother. She drives the same way she does everything else—competently and forcefully, with great nervous energy. She is a hard person to be relaxed with. He thinks it would be nice to get away from her for a while, nice to get away from the whole family. It would give him time to catch his breath long enough to find out who he is.

His mother notices his eyes on her. Her jaw juts out in its familiar, pugnacious expression, and she shoots a quick glance at him. "It will be good for you to have someone else around," she says. "You're getting very selfish."

An accusing note has crept into her voice. Brenton hunches his shoulders and looks out of the window without answering. Sometimes she seems to need to vent her irritation by pursuing him relentlessly until they have an all-out row. He hopes he can divert her with silence.

Huge gray grain silos flash past. He has a momentary vision of different silos, their tops opening and the sleek, pointed, unbelievable weapons sliding out with a whoosh up into the sky. He shuts his eyes and begins to count slowly.

Will he get to one hundred before the bombs start to fall?

Seventy-eight, seventy-nine . . .

The car swerves suddenly. He opens his eyes involuntarily. The landscape looks barren enough to have been blasted by a firestorm, but in fact it is the normal, everyday face of the peninsula, treeless and stony. Away to the right extend the mud flats of the gulf, the tide almost at full ebb. It is getting hot. Chris winds up her window and puts on the air conditioner.

"Don't you think that's true?" she challenges.

"What?" Brenton has forgotten what she was talking about.

"That you're getting very selfish."

He shrugs his shoulders. "I don't know!" The question of being selfish doesn't seem very relevant to him. If you're not going to live to grow up what difference does it make? Besides, selfishness has got to be relative; it all depends on your point of view. It seems to him the height of selfishness to pursue, as his parents do, your own comfortable existence while the human race rushes toward extinction all around you.

11

"BRENTON, stop fiddling with those dice!" Chris gives her son an exasperated look as the smooth-voiced PA divulges information: "Qantas flight from Perth, Singapore, Bahrain, Rome and London has arrived. Passengers are now disembarking. . . ."

Six and five. Brenton scoops the dice quickly up and composes his features in a welcoming grin.

"There she is!" Chris exclaims. Among the crowds of exuberant Europeans Brenton sees a small, dark-haired girl following the stewardess, clutching a flight bag. Her face is tanned and serious and she is screwing up her eyes, squinting a little as if she might be shortsighted. As they walk through the glass doors, the stewardess turns to say goodbye to someone, and the heavy shoulder bag hits the girl quite hard on the head. Brenton watches her. She flinches a little, but she is not fazed. She squares her shoulders and frowns a little more deeply. Now he can see that this is the girl who bit him in rage.

She sees Chris and Brenton. For a moment she looks panic-stricken. Then she smiles. The smile breaks up the precocious sternness of her face, crinkles her hazel eyes and makes dimples appear on either side of her mouth. He is not sorry he has to like her, especially since she only comes up to his shoulder.

"Hi!" he says and lets her have the full effect of the welcoming grin.

"How was the trip?" Chris says predictably, as she bends down to kiss Victoria.

20

12 THE TRIP *is a kaleidoscope of memories like a dream. At one moment she is saying a heart-chilling good-bye to her family at Kano airport in Nigeria, the next she is looking out of the window of the 747 and seeing thousands of meters below her the twinkling of small fires in the desert. Now she can feel Mrs. Stephenson's cheek against hers as they kiss good-bye in Rome, and now it is the smooth pillow and the red blanket, and she's trying to sleep on the plane. The engines drone on and on, and everything smells cold and stale. She's woken up when she wants to sleep and given food when she's not hungry, and when she's wide awake and starving all the lights are out and nobody moves for hours. At one airport a kind Chinese man shows her all the fabulous electronic gadgets, but she finds his accent hard to understand, and her face aches from smiling. A string of interchangeable flight attendants greet her, ask her identical friendly questions without waiting for the answers and give her coloring books as though she were six. She feels as though she has stepped outside her own body and is watching everything that happens like an unconcerned observer. She doesn't like it.*

13 "IT WAS OK," Victoria answers, forcing another smile for Chris and Brenton. But she is thinking, Why did it have to be Brenton? I wish Mick had come instead.

14 THE FALCON crosses the empty city and takes the road north.

"Do you remember it all, Vicky?" Chris asks her. The three of them are in the front seat, Brenton in the middle, Victoria next to the window.

"I thought I did. But it all looks completely different."

There seems to be too much of everything. Everything is too new, shiny and wealthy. The people's faces are too white and, in spite of the wealthiness, unhappy. She thought she was coming home. Now she realizes the place she left is home. And already she's feeling homesick!

"It's so different from Nigeria," she says helplessly.

"What's it like there?" Brenton asks curiously. "Is everybody starving?" He visualizes helpless black people, emaciated in the desert with the word APPEAL printed in red across them.

She knows what he is talking about because it is an image, along with beautiful brown babies and soldiers with machine guns, that she used to share. But the African people are no longer a series of clichéd images to her. They have become real people, as real as her own family, more real than the Trethewans.

"It's not like that," she tries to explain. "It's nothing like we used to see on TV over here before we went there. Things are bad, but not everything . . . some things are really great, better than here. . . ." Her voice trails away. "I can't really describe it," she finishes rather helplessly. "I've got some photos, I'll show them to you later."

"It must have been quite an experience for you," Chris remarks. "It's certainly made you grow up a lot. Are all the family all right? Simon was quite sick for a while, wasn't he?"

"He had an ear infection. Mum couldn't get hold of any antibiotics. He's all right now. They all are. Mum and Dad work really hard though. There's always so much to do, and it's hard getting anything done. The phones don't work and the electricity's always being cut off. But Mum's got her family planning clinic set up—and Dad thinks he's on the track of something really exciting. . . ."

Her voice fades away. It is strange talking about her parents. It makes her feel very far away from them, far away and suddenly grown-up.

"What does your dad do there?" Brenton asks.

"He's a plant geneticist, remember? He's trying to develop new strains of plants, peanuts in particular, that give a bigger crop and don't get spoiled by insects."

"Why does he have to go to Nigeria to do that?" Brenton looks sideways at her, puzzled.

"He thinks he can be more use there than here," Victoria replies rather distractedly, as though she is thinking of something else.

15 PETER HARE *tells the children at dinner. They are sitting at the table in their house in the hills. It's already dark, but the curtains are not yet drawn; the family likes to look out the window at the lights of the city spread out below.*

Victoria is nine, Simon seven. The whole family is startlingly alike, small-boned and dark-haired. Simon has his mother's blue eyes, Victoria her father's hazel ones.

"Mum and I have been thinking about things," her father says. The children eye him silently. Their parents are always thinking about things, with strong and not always welcome results.

"I've been offered a job in a country in Africa, and Mum and I think we should go there."

"What about us?" For a moment Victoria thinks the children will be left behind.

"We'd all go there," their mother says quickly. "But it will be for quite a long time. We'll have to sell the house."

"Will I have to go to a new school?" Simon says in alarm.

And Victoria asks, "What about Sparky and the cats?"

"We'll find homes for them," her mother assures her. "And there may not be any schools where we are. You'll have to do correspondence lessons."

"No school? Is there any television?" Simon's alarm is increasing rapidly.

"That's one of the reasons I want to go," their father says
24 *firmly. "I don't want you two growing up only in this society.*

I don't like it very much. I want you to see how other people live. All you're learning to value here is affluence and materialism. I want to use the skills I've been lucky enough to get helping other people, not just accumulating more things for myself. And your mother feels the same. She doesn't want to take private nursing jobs to put you through private schools like most of her friends have ended up doing."

Victoria and Simon exchange glances. They've heard it all before. It's part of their parents' strict philosophy, along with taking responsibility for yourself, being unselfish and not eating candy. They don't disagree with it, but sometimes it's hard work. Contemplating this new departure, Victoria sees herself giving a cup of cold water to a little black child. She likes black children; she thinks they are beautiful, much prettier than white children.

Another image comes into her mind, less comforting. A soldier with a machine gun stalks through a forest.

"Will there be a war there?" she asks, trying not to sound frightened.

"Of course not," her father says. "It's a very peaceful place."

16 HER HEAD has started to nod, and she opens her eyes with a jolt. Outside the window the suburbs are giving way to open countryside. On the left of the highway marshy water shimmers in the afternoon heat. For a moment she does not know where in the world she is.

"We're just going up the side of the gulf," Brenton ex-   **25** plains. "When we get to the top, we go down the other side—that's the peninsula."

"How long does it take?"

"A couple of hours."

Victoria presses her lips together to stop a sigh escaping. She looks out of the window, frowning. Her eyes blink rapidly. Her tongue comes out of her mouth and moistens her lips. She has been traveling for nearly two days; she doesn't see how she can get through another two hours.

"Let's stop and have a drink, Mum. Vicky's probably thirsty."

"We'll stop at Port Weston," Chris promises. "Are you feeling okay, Vicky? Not carsick?"

"Just exhausted," she admits.

"Did you get any sleep on the plane?"

"A bit. Not much. I saw something I've never seen before: the sun coming up over the whole world. It was marvelous."

17

FROM THE *window she can see beyond the wing of the plane to the edge of the world. It is fiercely delineated in orange, as though flames are blazing below the horizon of the starless sky. The orange becomes brighter and brighter, leaping upward into the heavens, tingeing the underbelly of the soft gray clouds with pink. She watches transfixed as dawn reclaims the world and night retreats, and a huge, round, dark-red sun shoulders its way above the horizon and begins its march across the sky.*

18 "YOU CAN go straight to bed when you get home." Chris tells Victoria. "I've put you in Mick's room."

"With him?" she asks, for at one time he was her best friend.

19 *TWO CHILDREN are crouching inside a cave. It's almost dark, and the sandstone is soft and damp. When Michael strikes a match, shadows jump grotesquely on the walls. He lights the candle in the jam jar and puts it down on the floor.*

"Got the scissors?"

Victoria nods and takes them out of her pocket. "I'll go first," she says. "Hold still." She carefully cuts a few strands of hair from his bangs. "Now you." She hands the scissors to him and sits back on her heels. The blades are cold against her forehead. They snip loudly.

"Don't take too much," she begs.

"I didn't!" Michael holds up the lock of black hair. "Now what?"

"Now we burn them and swear eternal friendship."

"Vicky, you do have some dumb ideas," he complains, but he holds out the black hair over the flame. It curls and singes, giving out an unpleasant, acrid smell.

"Ouch!" Michael lets go of the hair and it falls onto the flame, making the candle splutter and die.

"Our eternal friendship just went out," he says. "And I burned my fingers!"

"Aw, come on, Mick, light it again. I've got to do my bit."

The flame alight once more, Victoria burns the sandy hair. She breathes in the smoke and coughs. In a deep voice she intones, "By this sacrifice we swear eternal friendship to each other and this cave will forever be the witness. May the roof fall in if we break this pledge."

"Don't say things like that," he pleads, looking around nervously.

"You've got to say 'So be it!'" she hisses.

"So be it!" Michael whispers hurriedly. The smoke is making his eyes water.

20

"NO, MICHAEL's moved in with Brenton."

Victoria looks at Brenton. "Sorry!"

"You should be! He gets up at four in the morning to go slaughtering innocent fish. They've done nothing to deserve it and neither have I!"

"I don't mind sharing with Mick. I'll go fishing with him, like we used to when we stayed at the shack."

"We thought you'd rather have a room of your own," Chris offers.

"She means she doesn't think it's proper for you to share with Mick," Brenton explains gravely. "You might seduce
28 him!"

"Brenton!" his mother exclaims angrily. Victoria is silent. Before she went away, her friendships with boys like Michael were innocent and sexless. Now it seems different connotations may be put on them. She wonders if she knows how to handle that. Becoming wary, she retreats into politeness.

"It's very nice of you to have me," she says to Chris. "I hope it's not going to be too much trouble."

She already feels hopelessly indebted to them. From now on they will be her family. They will feed her, drive her around, buy her things, wake her up in the morning and put her to bed at night just like one of them. Why are they doing it? And why does it make her feel so uncomfortable, as if she has to be grateful all the time? It makes her feel like a victim.

21

"YOU WILL remember to be polite? And help Chris when she needs it?" Jenny Hare's calm plain face is worried as she packs her daughter's suitcase.

Victoria turns away from the window. She has been watching Lavinia's children playing with a puppy in the driveway. Outside, the African sun beats down, making the canna lilies and the salvia burn with bright, clashing reds and oranges. Inside the room it is dark and cool. The ceiling fan is turning lethargically. One of the blades is broken. It makes a slight, rhythmic clack, clack, clack.

Victoria nods without saying anything. She can't understand why she's not screaming, protesting, crying out that she doesn't want to go.

Don't send me away, she begs silently. Let me stay **29**

here with you and Dad and Simon. I don't want to leave you!

But she doesn't say it. She hasn't so far and she knows she's not going to. She accepts it as inevitable that she has to go away. There's nothing she can do about it.

Her mother closes the lid of the case and looks at her watch. "We've got half an hour before we have to leave. Do you want a drink? Something to eat?"

Victoria shakes her head.

22 SHE WISHES now she had had one last drink from her mother's hand. The car lurches to the left and pulls up in front of a roadhouse. Chris reaches over the seat for her bag. She gives Brenton a five-dollar bill. "Take Vicky in and get her something. I'm going to sit here and have a cigarette."

"Do you want a drink?"

"You can bring me some mineral water if they've got it."

Victoria follows Brenton, but inside there are too many things to choose from. The different colors, the noise and heat make her head start to swim. Brenton gets them each a Fanta. He puts one icy cold bottle into her hands.

"Go back to the car," he tells her. "I'll get Mum's mineral water."

When he slides into the front seat next to her, he puts something else in her hand. "Barley sugar. Glucose," he explains. "Just the thing for exhaustion."

Chris looks at him in surprise, her mouth pursed around **30** the straw of her drink.

"That was very thoughtful of you, Brenton."

"You needn't sound so amazed," he replies, and he winks at Victoria.

23

"HAVE YOU still got all your animals?" Victoria asks as they turn off the main road and begin to travel south down the peninsula.

"You know Mum! I think we've got even more than we had when you were last here."

"You had the cats, the lovely brown ones," she says, shifting the barley sugar from one side of her mouth to the other. "And all the funny chooks."

"Funny chooks! You mean Mrs. Trethewan's prize poultry. They've all had countless offspring. And we've branched out into goats. Anglo-Nubians. They're brown too, like the cats, with floppy ears. Nice looking."

"I hope you're going to help me look after them, Vicky," Chris says. "My children are a great disappointment to me; they aren't in the least bit interested in animals!"

"That's not true," Brenton argues. "I like the cats. The others are just too much work."

His mother gives him a scathing look. He rapidly changes the subject. "You remember the shack, Vicky?"

"Of course I do!" Her family had spent their holidays there for as long as she could remember. It belonged to the Trethewans but was on the opposite side of the road from their house, on top of the cliff.

"It's not ours anymore. One of Dad's cousins bought it. They've put up a hideous great galvanized iron fence and **31** modernized it inside. Ruined it. We should never have sold it, Mum."

"Question of money, I'm afraid," she replies. "When we got the boat we had nothing left for the mortgage."

"Have you got a new boat?" Vicky asks. "What happened to the old one?"

Brenton is about to say something but his mother interrupts. "Don't upset Vicky with that now. There are the goats," she says, changing the subject with artificial enthusiasm as they turn into the driveway. "In the paddock on the left, under the trees."

Victoria stares at them enraptured. "Aren't they beautiful! We had a pet goat in Kano," she adds, "but we had to eat it."

Chris laughs. "Goat meat is very tasty."

"Yuck!" Brenton exclaims. "Don't you dare give it to us!"

"If we get male kids we'll probably have to kill and eat them," his mother remarks. "There's not much of a market for them, and we can't keep them all as pets."

"That's the trouble with breeding animals," Brenton says. "You always end up having to kill them for some reason or another. Speaking as a male kid myself, I'd like to make a protest!"

Victoria is absorbing the familiar surroundings. They have hardly changed at all in two and a half years, except that everything seems to have shrunk slightly. At the end of the driveway stands the old stone house with its roof of dull pewter-colored tin. On the left is the almond orchard, the fruit hard and green. Underneath the trees about two dozen hens of varying colors and sizes are scratching. Four different roosters are outcrowing each other from their separate pens.

32   "What are the lovely fluffy white ones?" Vicky asks.

"Silky bantams," Chris replies. "I haven't had them very long, but they're far and away my favorites. They're so cute looking and they're brilliant little mothers."

"I'd love to help you with them," Vicky exclaims enthusiastically. "I love animals."

Chris drives around to the back of the house. The car stops and she switches off the ignition. "Yes, I remember you and Simon always were keen on animals. It seemed such a waste that you two had to live in the city, while our children, living in the country, never cared for them much."

As she gets slowly out of the car Victoria is thinking of other animals that she still thinks of as hers, even though it's two years since she's seen them.

24

PETER HARE *keeps the whole family fired up with enthusiasm, but there are a lot of bad things about going away, and saying good-bye to the dog, Sparky, and the two cats, Claude and Sam, is the worst thing of all.*

Sparky is going to live with a colleague of her father's, who comes to fetch him in a car.

"He hasn't got any children," Victoria worries. "Sparky'll have no one to look after." The dog is part Border collie and he needs things to care for. When he's put in the car he whines, and the last they see of him is his head looking anxiously back at them, his tongue hanging out.

The cats are staying with the house. The people who have bought it say they are happy to have them.

"They'll be fine," her mother tells Victoria. **33**

"But they won't know where we are," she protests, and when it's time to go, catlike they have vanished from the scene. All the way to the airport Victoria keeps saying, "I just wanted to see them once more." By the time they get on the plane she is pale and tearful.

25

SHE CAN feel tears in her eyes as Brenton says again, "I like the cats."

The cats have heard the car and come out yowling in welcome. They have huge amber eyes and short, dense, chocolate-brown fur. Brenton picks up Tang and drapes him over his shoulder. Tang turns his head around and licks the boy lovingly and raspingly on the ear. Ting is weaving a figure-eight pattern between Brenton's legs. Victoria bends down to stroke her. The cat sniffs disdainfully at her fingers and then graciously allows her to pat her head.

Chris shuts the car door and stretches her arms with a sigh of relief. She is happy to be home, happy that Victoria has arrived safely, happy that Brenton has behaved like a reasonable human being for several hours.

"Come inside, Vicky," she says. "Do you want something to eat, or do you want to go straight to bed?"

26 NOW it is night again where Victoria finds herself, but it's not nighttime for her; it's morning and she can't understand, when she opens her eyes suddenly in the strange room, why it is so dark.

It is around the time of false dawn. Outside, a rooster crows and from a distant farm a dog barks. Her mouth is dry; her tongue is huge. She can barely swallow.

27 HER MOTHER *keeps a flask of chilled locally made fruit cordial in the kitchen. When you open the lid ice cubes chink together enticingly. It's the most refreshing drink in the world.*

28 THE CORDIAL is *there* and Victoria is here with thousands of miles between them. She gives a long shuddering sigh which turns into a sob, and once the sobs have started she can't stop them. She buries her head under the pillow, until she thinks she's going to suffocate, and the tears just won't stop trickling out, and her throat won't stop hurting, and it keeps on being **35**

dark nighttime when it should be morning, and she keeps repeating to herself with a sort of horrified amazement, "I didn't know it was going to be this bad."

Then she remembers with total clarity someone putting an ice-cold bottle of Fanta into her hands, and she hears Brenton saying, "Barley sugar. Glucose. Just the thing for exhaustion."

The packet is on the table next to the bed. Her fingers close gratefully over a candy, unwrap the waxy paper, slip the round, comforting, sweet thing into her mouth. For a moment she can't breathe; her mouth is full of barley sugar, and her nose is blocked up from the tears. What a funny way to go, she thinks hysterically. Choked to death by a piece of barley sugar.

Then her nose clears and her breathing calms down. She eats four more of them and falls asleep just as the real dawn is breaking.

 "THIS IS Planet Earth calling Victoria! Come in Victoria!"

She opens her eyes abruptly. She sits up, looking distractedly around the strange room. Michael Trethewan is regarding her warily from the door.

"Mum sent me to see if you're awake. She says you've got to get up, so you can get into the right routine as quickly as possible. And she told me to ask you if you wanted to come down to the beach with me."

He doesn't sound enthusiastic about the idea. Victoria
36 looks at him defensively. She wants to go with him, to

reestablish the old easygoing friendship they used to have, but she has a streak of pride and independence that makes her reluctant to foist herself on him.

"You go ahead," she says. "I can come down later when I've had breakfast."

His face brightens and he gives her a smile of relief. "OK! See you later then."

He shouts to his mother as he leaves the room, "She doesn't want to come!"

The screen door slams. His footsteps thud over the wooden veranda and down the steps.

30 THE HOUSE is silent. It's as if she's alone on the planet. Feeling abandoned, Victoria gets out of bed and crosses the room to the window. From it she can see the orchard, the poultry runs and the paddock. Someone in blue jeans and a white top is walking among the goats. She screws up her eyes, trying to see who it is.

Chris. Should she be helping her?

Victoria gets dressed. It is frustrating. The clothes she wants to wear seem to have disappeared, and the suitcase her mother packed so neatly has mysteriously jumbled itself up. Finally she pins down a pair of shorts and a T-shirt, and clad in these she heads for the kitchen.

As she comes through one door, Chris Trethewan comes through the other, her hands full of eggs.

"Didn't take a basket," she explains as she carefully puts them down on the counter. "Brenton's meant to collect the **37** eggs but he forgot this morning, typically. Forgot or chose not to remember. He wanted to go over to Barbridge with Shelley and Jason, and they didn't want to hang about. And Mick's taken off too. I'm afraid they've rather abandoned you."

"It doesn't matter," Victoria says untruthfully. "I can look after myself." Chris smiles in relief. Whether it's true or not, it's what she wants to hear.

"I'm sure you can! You always were a very independent and sensible girl. Now what about breakfast? Then you can go and have a look around."

31 SHE HAS eaten breakfast. She has done the washing up. She has made her bed. She has put away her clothes. The suitcase is unpacked. She is no longer on the way to somewhere: she is truly here. A photo of her parents and Simon looks back at her from the bedside table, establishing them as distant, absent. What is she going to do now?

32 CHRIS IS in her sewing room at the back of the house, off the laundry room. This is her haven, the place she retreats to. Victoria stands in the door and observes her.

There are baskets full of materials and wool and decorations and craft works in various stages of design and construction. It's like a treasure house, full of color and light, haphazard but not disorderly. Chris sits in the center of it, looking both at home and magical as though she might suddenly cast a spell. The morning sunlight pours in through the window and makes her hair look very blonde. It reminds Victoria of a fairy story, of someone spinning gold.

"What are you doing?"

Chris is twisting thick blue wool through a standing loom. "I should be making Christmas decorations, but I just feel like working on this for a bit. It always calms me down after I've had a row with my son."

Victoria is silent for a moment while she wonders which son and what the row was about. She feels too much of an outsider to inquire about it, so she asks about the weaving instead.

"What is it?"

"It's going to be a wall hanging. I make quite a few of them. You've probably noticed them all over the house."

"It's lovely!" The interwoven patterns—blue, green and a sunny gold—lift Victoria's spirits. They glow with the colors of the summer sea and sky. Chris's face is calm and happy as she works.

"I didn't know that you did this sort of thing."

"I suppose I've only started making them in the last couple of years. I found I really liked it—and people are always ready to buy them so I must be quite good at it. Geoff doesn't think much of it," she adds. "He'd rather I was doing something practical like going back to nursing."

"But these make money too, don't they?"

Chris laughs. "The prices I can sell them for only just cover the materials. They're never going to pay back the **39** mortgage. Oh well!" She picks up a hank of wool, holds it against the work, tosses it back in the basket and selects another. Pulling out a strand, she begins to weave it in. "I may as well keep on doing it as long as I can." She smiles cheerfully at Victoria. "Why don't you go and have a look around outside?"

33 IT'S A dismissal, but Victoria doesn't mind. She feels she can go back to the room full of colors some other time, and then she will be allowed to stay longer, even to start making things there herself. As she slips out the kitchen door her head is full of the blue and green and gold of the wall hanging, and she sees the whole landscape in the same clear tones.

The shack calls her. She spent so many holidays there she has always felt it belongs to her. She walks down the driveway, under the dappled shade of the poplars, and crosses the road.

The galvanized fence runs stark across the frontage of the land. It's unpleasant to think that land, shack and path down to the sea now belong to someone else. Vicky ducks under the barbed wire in the neighboring field and climbs the stone wall that separates the field from the shack.

The shack is an original stone cottage with extra rooms tacked on the back. Between the wall where Vicky is balanced and the side wall of the house stands a row of pine trees, planted as a windbreak, their tops flattened into a slope by the southwesterly gales. A newish Toyota 4WD is parked just inside the gate, and fishing gear is piled on the

outside table. Two wetsuits hang on the clothesline.

Just beyond, Vicky can see the path that leads to the beach. She feels like staking a claim to her former territory. She considers the new people intruders. So she jumps off the wall and runs across the yard, ducks under the clothesline and takes the path.

At the same moment something large and dark hurls itself out of the shade where it was lying and hurtles down toward her with a ferocious volley of barking. It is a huge black and brown rottweiler, and luckily for Victoria it's on the end of a chain. The chain, unraveling, makes as much noise as the dog. With a jolt the animal comes to the end of its tether and dances on its hind legs, barking and snarling. Victoria has time to notice that foam is actually coming out of its mouth, and then she runs for her life across the top of the cliff and down the gully.

It is a rough terrain. Shards of rock and stones bruise her feet through her sandals; tumbleweed and burrs whip and scratch at her bare legs. Her heart is beating fast from surprise, but she's not actually frightened. She's rather elated at having got past the barking dog and the shack without being seen, but the elation is short-lived, for as she half-slithers, half-jumps down the rough steps that have been cut out of the clayey rock of the cliff face, she nearly crashes into someone who is coming up.

"Hey!" The voice is outraged and commanding, and Victoria, who is obedient by nature, stops. Almost at once she wishes she hadn't.

"What the hell do you think you're doing? This is private property." The speaker is a woman who could be any age between thirty-five and fifty. She is wearing a red swimsuit, with a tracksuit top of not quite the same red over her shoulders. She's not tall, but she's firm-muscled, and she looks tough and powerful. Her hair, eyes and skin are all the same color, bleached brown like the shale of the cliff. **41**

She would be good-looking but for a certain set of the mouth and an expression in the eyes that suggest she is carrying rage and pain around with her like darkness.

Victoria would give anything to escape, but since she can't she reckons it's expedient to be polite. "I'm staying at the Trethewans' " (this establishes her as a local) "and I'm just going down to the beach."

The woman stares at her. She is not mollified in the least. If anything her face hardens.

"You'd think they'd bloody well know better," she hisses. "Letting a bloody kid wander around the place on her own."

"Oh, I know my way around," Vicky interrupts. "We used to stay here. . . ."

"You know you were lucky the dog was chained up? If he'd been loose you'd have lost your arm by now. He's trained to go for intruders. He never lets go."

Victoria can feel unnerving waves of anxiety and hostility coming from the woman. In spite of herself she shivers.

"I'm sorry," she says. "I won't do it again. Is it all right if I just go on to the beach?" Not waiting for an answer she jumps rapidly down the remaining steps and starts to walk purposefully along the shore. But the woman pursues her.

"You want to be careful," she shouts. "See that net?"

It lies lifeless on the sand as the tide ebbs away from it.

"Stay away from that when you're swimming. Sharks come up around it to get the fish; they could tear you apart. And mind where you step, there're stingrays on the bottom."

"I'll be careful," Victoria promises. She knows the beach like the back of her hand. Until her family went away, she swam here every summer. She knows it's not dangerous. All the same the woman is having a strange effect on her. Not thinking what she's doing she puts her foot into a pool

42 and turns over a rock with her toe.

"Don't do that!" the woman cries out. "Sheesh!" she groans. "Haven't you ever heard of the blue-ringed octopus? They hide under these rocks. One bite and you've snuffed it. You'd be dead before you reached the hospital."

Victoria is desperately wishing she could get away from this person, who she thinks must be a little crazy. At the same time she can feel herself starting to see the funny side of the conversation. She bends down to take her sandals off.

"Don't go in the water without shoes on," the woman goes on relentlessly. "There's razor shells in there so sharp they'd cut your feet off!"

Halfway through unbuckling her sandals Vicky looks up in disbelief.

"It's true! My uncle cut his foot off on a razor shell, clean through!"

"How awful for him," Vicky says, but she stands up with her sandals not on her feet but in her hand, and she has a mad uncontrollable desire to giggle.

"Don't you dare laugh at me, you little turd!"

The words hit Victoria almost physically. The attack is so unexpected it leaves her shaking. She no longer has any desire to laugh. Her only desire is to get away. Her face is hot and her eyes are pricking. She turns and almost runs away down the beach.

The woman stares after her, a curious mixture of malice and concern on her face. "And stay away from the caves!" she calls out. "Don't expect us to dig you out if you get yourself buried alive!"

34 *BURIED ALIVE!* the echo rolls back to Victoria as she stumbles along the shore. It could be a warning or a curse.

Her face is burning, not from the sun, but from anger and humiliation. Something that used to belong to her and that she held precious has been destroyed. The beach has lost its blue and golden beauty and now looks only ugly. Slowing down to a walk, breathing heavily, Victoria wipes the back of her hand across her eyes, and stares at the flat, muddy expanse of shallow pools and seaweed, smelling of rot in the sun, rendered even uglier by broken glass on the foreshore and, below the cliff, the old garbage dump where generations of tires, mattresses and oil drums have been thrown out.

35 FROM THE cliff around the old dump a flock of pigeons rises suddenly, though Victoria can neither see nor hear anything that would have startled them. Their wings smack as they trace a wide semi-circle over her head and return to their home in the rocks. Below where they are settling she can see the black mouths of the caves, looking as though some giant maggot has been chewing holes in the cliff. Ominous. She remembers the **44** times she and Michael explored them and hid from Brenton in them, and she shivers. Either she has caught fear from the woman on the beach or she is more of a coward than she was when she was nine. Nothing would make her venture into them now. She remembers with familiar dread the local story of two boys who were buried in a landslide twenty years ago. Their bodies were never found.

There is no one in sight in either direction, but Victoria is feeling absurdly self-conscious, as though everything she does is being observed. She realizes with a shock that, perhaps for the first time in her life, her parents do not know exactly where she is. Up till now they have always been around to keep an eye on her. Now she is unprotected. She has lost her shield. She is out in the open. She glances quickly around. The beach seems empty, but something catches her eye down by the caves. She looks away out to sea, where the tide is sluggishly retreating toward the east, and then back again. This time she is sure of it; something moved just inside the entrance to one of the caves.

Immediately she suspects it's Michael, hiding there, spying on her. She decides to creep up on him and surprise him.

She runs out toward the sea, jumping over rock pools and squishing sea grapes, until she is well past the caves; then she doubles back, close to the cliff now, creeping quietly, holding her breath. She has forgotten her fears and her self-consciousness. She is intent on the game she is playing.

Feet crunch on the shale. She ducks quickly behind a rock and flattens herself up against the cliff. A complete stranger comes quietly, almost furtively, around the corner.

36 FEELING like an idiot, Victoria jumps up, brushing shells and sand from her clothes and legs. Fancy being caught playing games like a little kid! She doesn't look up; she expects the stranger to walk on past her. She is fervently wishing he would, but when after what seems like forever he doesn't, she raises her eyes and looks at him angrily.

His appearance startles her. His skin is dark brown; he has a lot of brown wiry hair; and his eyes are as black as olives. He is taller than she is, but so thin he seems elongated, and she can't decide if he is a very small adult or a very self-possessed child. Then she realizes that she's not sure if she's right in thinking of the person before her as *he*. But the self-possession, and something about the way he is standing, make her think after all that she is.

She doesn't like the way he is staring intently at her, running his eyes over her as though he is cataloguing everything about her. Then he smiles at her in a way that immediately makes her feel very nervous and, still studying her as though she is an interesting biological specimen, he says something to her that she can't understand.

While half her mind is grappling with the unfamiliar sounds, the other half is taking in the fact that the boy is wearing rather unusual clothes—a loose-fitting, all-in-one garment like very exotic overalls, made of a shimmery material that adapts itself perfectly to the background. She notices quite clearly that the leg closest to the cliff is darker, while the other leg is lighter, with patterns on it just like the sand behind it.

46

What's going on? she thinks wildly. This beach is swarming with weirdos!

The dark-skinned boy says something else, more insistently. Even though she can't understand a word, there's a sort of bossiness about what he's saying that gets under her skin.

"Go away!" she says loudly. "Get lost!"

His first reaction is to flinch at the anger in her voice, but he quickly recovers himself and seems almost pleased. He smiles and nods encouragingly. He is holding a small, silvery, flat object in one hand, and he now lifts it up and stares at it. After a few seconds he lowers it and says in a perfect imitation of her voice, "Go away! Get lost!" He gives a little nod of satisfaction and makes a sort of beckoning gesture to Victoria, indicating that she should say something else.

"Oh, for heaven's sake!" she says in exasperation. She tries to walk away, but he is standing in her path.

"Oh, for heaven's sake!" he repeats, so accurately that she stands and stares at him.

For the second time that morning she goes hot with humiliation. Tiredness and jet lag are catching up with her. The whole scene suddenly becomes unreal, as though she's watching it on film. She has a rapid memory of the blue-green weaving.

That's where she wants to be. She turns to bolt for home.

He speaks again urgently and grasps her arm to detain her.

"Let go!" Vicky says desperately, shaking her arm hard, but he has let go almost as quickly as he grabbed her, a look of disgust on his dark face.

"Ugh!" he exclaims. Shuddering as if in horror, he unslings from his back a pack that Victoria had not noticed before. It is made out of the same shimmery material as **47** the overalls, and it opens soundlessly at the boy's touch. He takes something out of it and offers it to her.

She has never seen anything so pretty. It amazes and delights her. She can't quite make out what it is, so she takes a step closer. The sunlight glints and sparkles off its many cut facets, and it picks up and reflects the blue of the sky and the now distant sea. The boy holds it out enticingly and smiles.

Victoria forgets all she has ever been told about not accepting gifts from strangers. She feels she has simply got to hold it, whatever it is, in her hand. As she takes it she realizes it is a necklace, though she can't figure out what the beads are made of or how they are strung together. She's never seen or felt anything like it in her life. It is smoother and colder than glass, heavier and clearer than plastic. The colors glow and sparkle and change as if they are alive. She loves it. She lifts it up and puts it around her neck.

"Thanks," she says awkwardly.

The boy nods and gives her another of his rather unnerving smiles.

"Thanks," he repeats several times. Then he holds out his hands, palms up, and looks at her questioningly.

Gee, I suppose I ought to give him something back, Victoria thinks. She searches in her pockets but she hasn't got anything with her except two tissues, clean ones, luckily, and the remains of the packet of barley sugar. They don't seem to be a very good exchange for the fantastic necklace. She shows them to the boy.

"That's all I've got. I could bring you something later."

A very strange look crosses his face, a blend of disappointment, disbelief, anger and alarm. He takes the tissues and looks at them carefully, unfolding them and feeling them between his fingers. Then he takes one of the barley sugars, unwraps it and studies it. He shakes his head and sighs.

"You eat it," Victoria says loudly, and when he makes no response she takes one herself, unwraps it and puts it in her mouth.

Another look of horror crosses his face. He drops the barley sugar, and shakes his head violently, waving his hands in front of his chest and stepping back as though she is going to force-feed him.

Since she has put on the necklace Victoria is no longer frightened, just fascinated. "Stay here," she says. "I'll go and get something for you." He repeats the words after her perfectly, but his face remains questioning.

She points at the sun and then to the horizon where the sun will be later in the day. "Me go now!" she says, tapping herself on the chest and gesturing away down the beach. "Me come back!" She taps herself again and points to the ground at their feet. Then she repeats the sun and horizon routine.

The boy seems to understand, but he does not agree. He shakes his head, points to himself, points back into the cave and waves. She is still puzzling this one out when she hears a shout.

"Vicky!"

Away down the beach, toward the township, a small figure is waving its arms and calling. She can't quite see who it is but she thinks it might be Michael.

"Vicky!"

The stranger speaks again. "Vicky?"

It is peculiar to hear her name spoken by him. It's as though he has named her for the first time. She exists, independent of family and home. She has never been so acutely aware of it before.

"Vicky," she confirms and grins at him. "What's your name? You?" She makes a gesture toward him.

Tapping himself on the chest he repeats the same word several times. It seems to have a number of consonants in a very small space.

"Cal?" she hazards. He laughs and shrugs as though to say, "Near enough."

"I'm going now, Cal," Victoria says firmly. Conversation without words is exhausting, and Michael is getting closer. "Good-bye." She waves as she says this and he waves too. "Good-bye," he repeats in her voice. "Good-bye, Vicky."

She turns once as she walks away. She can no longer see the stranger. Either he is camouflaged against the cliff or he has gone back into the cave. She raises a hand and waves just in case. Then she tucks the necklace inside her shirt and begins to run.

37 THE SHAPE Victoria is running toward is also dark and elongated by distance, but as she gets closer it resolves itself into stocky, sandy-haired Michael. She is relieved and delighted to see him. The two bizarre daytime encounters have unnerved her as much as the unexpected nighttime homesickness.

"Mum sent me to look for you." He doesn't say it with tremendous enthusiasm, but at least he is indisputably normal.

"Can we go back through the town?" Vicky asks.

"Do we have to? We'll be late for lunch."

50   "I don't want to go past the shack again."

Michael has not looked at her directly yet. Now he does. "Is something up?"

"A woman from the shack talked to me . . ." Victoria begins hesitantly, and understanding spreads over Michael's freckled face. He shakes his head expressively.

"That's Pam. She's married to Dad's cousin that bought the old place." He pauses for a moment and then continues rather awkwardly, suddenly serious. "Their son drowned here last year. He and a friend of his took the dinghy out too far and got caught in a squall. It was in the papers."

"How awful!" Vicky shivers and looks out over the waters of the gulf, now, at low tide, so far away and tranquil. "Did you know them?"

"Not very well. They hadn't been here very long. He was called Brett—he was sixteen."

"That explains why she was so weird! No wonder she kept telling me how dangerous everything was."

"Yeah, she does that to everybody. Did she warn you about the blue-ringed octopus?"

Vicky doesn't want to think about poor dead Brett, or his sad still-alive mother, and the only way to stop herself is to go off on a jokey tangent.

"The blue-ringed octopus bites your foot off. No, hang about, I've got it wrong. It's the sharks that bite your foot off. The blue-ringed octopus drags you into the caves and buries you alive."

"Penbowie is a dangerous place," Michael intones, happy to follow her lead. "You took your life in your hands when you came here."

"Little did her parents think," Victoria announces in sinister tones, "when they dispatched their only daughter to the sleepy seaside town . . ."

"Just when she thought it was safe to go on the beach **51** again!" Michael adds. They both begin to giggle. The giggling, plus the fact that it is Michael she's giggling with, takes the humiliating sting out of Victoria's encounter with the unhappy woman and helps to lay Brett's ghost to rest.

"Come on, I'll race you to the wall."

Two years ago Vicky had been as fast as Michael. Now he easily outdistances her.

"It's not fair," she pants as she comes up to the seawall alongside the jetty. "Your legs have grown too long!"

Scorning the steps Michael vaults up onto the wall.

"I bet I can do that!" Vicky spring up, misses her footing and falls in a heap on the sand, setting off the giggling all over again. "I can do it, I can do it!" she keeps saying, refusing Michael's outstretched arm, taking longer and longer run-ups, but never quite managing to get to the top of the wall. Finally exclaiming, "Oh, I give up!" she takes his hand and pulls hard. He pulls back and for a moment they are perfectly balanced. Victoria however has gravity on her side. Michael loses his balance and falls on top of her in the sand.

"You idiot!" he yells. "I'm going to punish you now. The death of a thousand drops!" He scoops up a handful of sand and lets a tiny amount fall on her face. She wriggles and splutters. The strange beads flash.

"What's this, Vicky?"

"Let me up and I'll show you."

He gets off her and Victoria scrambles to her feet, dusting her clothes and hair. She makes a face and spits sand out. Michael is remembering that one of the things he used to like about this girl is that she never cried or made a fuss. It makes him feel a lot more charitable toward her. Vicky **52** glances at him sideways as she takes the necklace from her neck and gives it to him. They smile tentatively but directly at each other.

The necklace flashes again as Michael takes it. "Wow!" he exclaims. "Did you get it in Nigeria?"

"A boy just gave it to me on the beach."

"Who?"

"I don't know, I'd never seen him before."

"I didn't see you talking to anyone," Michael says in surprise.

"He was wearing camouflage."

"Camouflage?"

"Yeah, he was an alien." She says it just to maintain the jokey relationship with Michael that has started up again so promisingly, but as soon as it's said she has a terrifying feeling it may be the truth. "He had funny clothes on that merge with the background," she continues. "That's why you couldn't see him."

Michael is prepared to go along with the joke. "He'd traveled light-years in time and space, I suppose, from a galaxy far, far away!"

"Something like that," she agrees, perplexed.

"Bringing a message of peace and hope for the human race?"

"He might have been. I couldn't understand a word he was saying."

It no longer sounds to Michael as if she is joking. He looks closely at the necklace. It is disturbingly alien, unlike anything he has ever seen.

"You're not serious, are you?"

"Micky, I don't know. It was so weird."

He hands the necklace back to her. "Come on, we must get home. Mum'll throw a fit."

He is silent for a while as they walk past the one shop **53** and one hotel which, with the old Literary Institute and a few houses, make up the township of Penbowie, but he is still puzzling over what she said, and as they take the road home he suggests, "Someone was having you on. It must have been a TV stunt. They probably had hidden cameras. You'll see yourself on TV next week looking like an idiot."

"Come off it! Where are the cameras? And why do it on a deserted beach where there's no one around but a couple of kids?"

"I bet it's something to do with TV," Michael persists. "Probably a commercial."

The open, yellowing countryside stretches away from them. The sky is high and huge. Victoria says slowly, "I told him I'd go back later. I want to take him something in return for the necklace."

"I'd better come with you. In case he turns out to be a pervert and murders you."

She is remembering how he looked. "I don't think he is a pervert."

"You can never tell," Michael assures her wisely. "The ones that don't look it are the worst. I'll come anyway. I want to have a look at him if he's still there. Then I can get on TV too."

"Hey!" Vicky turns to him and grabs his arm. "Don't tell the others. Let's keep it a secret."

"I'm not telling anyone," he replies swiftly. "Imagine how they'd laugh!" He looks rather self-consciously at her hand on his arm and eases himself away from her. Then he makes a point of walking rather quickly, so she is kept a couple of paces behind him.

38 WITH a squeal of brakes and a *toot toot* a car draws up alongside the two of them, making both jump. Shelley, bare arm on the window frame, hair dark with water, salt and sand, calls out, "Hop in, kids. We'll give you a lift."

"Where've you been?" Michael asks as they climb in the back with Brenton.

"Over to Barbridge Bay."

"Surf any good?"

"Lousy" and "not bad" Brenton and Shelley say together.

"What did you think, Jase?"

Jason Snedman, who is driving, looks in the rearview mirror at Mick and then back at the road. "I have to agree with Shelley!" he says. "It's more than my life's worth not to!"

"Not true," Shelley squeals, hitting him playfully on the arm. "I like a fella with a mind of his own."

Jason puts his arm around her and hugs her. She leans across and tries to kiss him on the mouth. Michael and Brenton groan in unison. "Cut it out! Censored! This vehicle is G rated!"

"Shut up!" Shelley says cheerfully. "What on earth will Vicky think of you? Jason, this is Vicky Hare. She's going to be staying with us for the holidays. You've probably seen her before. Her family used to come and stay at the shack."

"Hi, Vicky!" Jason says without looking around.

"Hi," she replies to the back of his head. She is thinking it was in another era, about a hundred years ago, that she **55** used to come here on holidays with her family, an era before people grew up and had boyfriends or got themselves drowned.

"Is Dad home?" Shelley asks Michael.

"I dunno. I've been out most of the morning. I thought he was going to take the boat out. Why?"

"Someone's vandalized the hospital," she announces dramatically.

"No! What'd they do?"

"Graffiti job. Decorated the entire side wall."

"Not the new building?" Michael is aghast.

"Yeah," Shelley says with the delight that comes from imparting really shocking news.

"Dad'll bust a gut," Michael says in awe. "Who do you reckon did it?"

"Must have been someone from the city," Jason answers. "No one local would do something like that."

"What did they write?"

"It's a real art job," Brenton puts in. "I think it rather improves the place. It's in orange and green, rap style, and it says *Dead End*—it's quite funny really when you think it's on the wall of the Terminal Care Unit."

"Funny!" Shelley exclaims. "You've got a sick sense of humor!"

"Brent may think it's artistic." Jason addresses only her. "It's still vandalism."

"Brenton!" says Brenton.

"What?"

"You called me Brent," he points out. "That's not my name."

"Sorry, *Brenton*," Jason says, exchanging looks with Shelley and grinning. "I was going to ask you if you wanted to **56** drive," he adds.

"I do," Brenton replies swiftly.

"Bad luck!" Jason says. "Only nonfussy people are allowed to drive my car."

"Can I?" Michael asks hopefully.

"Next time," Jason promises as he pulls up outside the Trethewans' house.

"Jason lets the boys practice driving sometimes," Shelley explains to Victoria as they get out of the car. "You'll have to give Vicky a turn too, Jase."

"*Jason!*" Michael reminds her. Victoria follows them into the house. They are all talking at the tops of their voices and she feels tiny and insubstantial next to them. She feels like telling them that her father has let her drive his car, but she doesn't think they will hear her, they are so full of confidence and energy. With an almost audible click, everything around her takes on the unreal, inconsequential coloring of a dream. As she trails into the kitchen after the others Chris casts a professional nurse's eye over her.

"Vicky, eat lunch and then lie down. You look absolutely exhausted."

39 VICTORIA opens her eyes with a huge effort. Magpies are warbling in the paddock and it feels as if it should be morning, but the light is all wrong.

Chris is looking at her from the door of the bedroom. "Vicky, I think you should get up now. I hate to wake you, but you must get into the right time as soon as possible. **57**

Otherwise you'll just wake up in the middle of the night and be exhausted again tomorrow."

"What time is it?"

"Half-past five. We're going to eat in about an hour."

Victoria drags herself out of bed, throat dry, limbs heavy, and goes and stands in the shower, letting the warm water run over her in a sort of trance. While she is standing there, thinking vaguely about different showers she has known, she remembers the boy on the beach. She wonders if he is waiting for her, or if she just dreamed about him. She turns off the shower, wraps her towel around her and, making sure no one is looking, scuttles back to her room.

Before she went to sleep she took the necklace off and hid it under her pillow. It is still there, unlikely enough to be a dream, but definitely real in her hand. The rays of light from the evening sun make it shimmer with a pink, electric, unearthly glow. The beads have an unexpected coldness that suggests ice. She puts it around her neck and looks at herself in the mirror. It glows pink and shimmery against her brown skin. It not only makes her look better, it makes her feel better too. Victoria thinks it is marvelous, but she's not sure what she thinks about the person who gave it to her. She doesn't particularly feel like going back to see him, but because she said she would she feels she should. Unable to make up her mind what to do, she dresses and goes to look for Michael.

The noise of a television leads her to the family room, but Michael is not there, only Brenton, curled up in a beanbag chair, his eyes fixed on the screen.

"What are you watching, Brenton?"

"Old video clips," he replies briefly.

"What's the song?"

58   " 'Walk of Life'—Dire Straits. Haven't you heard it?"

"I've heard of Dire Straits, but I don't know this one."

"Hasn't it penetrated darkest Africa?"

"They don't have much pop music on the radio there— lots of local songs and things in French and Arabic. And 'We are the World.' I've heard that."

"Who hasn't?" he returns rather scornfully. "Walk of Life" comes to an end. Another clip follows.

"Do you know where Mick is?"

"No." That seems to be all Brenton is going to say, but he surprises her a few seconds later by giving her a flashing smile and saying, "I mean, I'm sorry, I don't know where he is!"

The effect is unnerving, and Victoria is wondering what to say next when the door opens spookily by itself and one of the Burmese cats walks in. It fixes Brenton with an amber stare and opens its mouth wide. Talking to him imploringly it crosses the room and jumps on top of him, continuing to stare fixedly at him and talk in its amazing fractured, incomprehensible voice.

"Move your head, Tang! I can't see the TV." Brenton pushes the small bony brown head down and scratches it gently behind the ears. The cat begins to purr loudly, but it doesn't want to have its head down, it wants to have it up so it can look Brenton in the eye and speak lovingly to him. "Mraaaooow," it says, and begins to lick his face methodically.

"What does he want?" Vicky asks.

"He wants me to feed him," Brenton replies in between licks. "He'll sit on me and pester me till I do. Come on, then, you monster cat." He uncurls himself from the bean-bag, drapes Tang over his shoulder and goes toward the kitchen. The cat clings onto his T-shirt, taking rapid licks at his ear.

Victoria follows them. In the kitchen the female cat is sitting on the floor by the plastic bowls, her paws tucked underneath her, her eyes half closed. She gets up with a yawn that shows her pink mouth and her sharp white teeth and begins to weave between Brenton's legs. "Get out of the way," he scolds, as he nearly trips over her, but he says it gently.

"Aren't they gorgeous!" Vicky bends down and strokes Ting on her smooth brown head. "They look like Egyptian cats, long necks and big ears."

"That's what I think," Brenton agrees. "They ought to be living in temples, being worshiped." He is getting the meat out of the fridge. Tang steadies himself on his shoulder and leaps to the floor.

"Ouch!" Brenton exclaims. "He always puts his claws in!"

"It's bleeding," Vicky remarks. A tiny patch of blood is spreading thread by thread through the white material of Brenton's shirt. He pulls it away from his neck and inspects the wound.

"Look!" His shoulders are covered in scratches, some new, some faint scars.

"You look as though you've been tortured!"

"Yeah, Rambo. Though I suppose that hasn't penetrated the dark continent either."

"Everyone's heard of *Rambo*! But my parents wouldn't let us see it!"

"It's Mick and Danny's favorite movie. They've seen it about twenty times."

40 HE'S wondering if he can put into words how much he despises Rambo when the outside door opens and his mother comes swiftly into the kitchen. "Brenton, can you please feed the animals? I want to get dinner started."

"I just fed the cats," he argues, "I've done my share. Ask one of the others."

"Mick's still down at Danny's and Shelley's getting dressed to go out."

"Well, I'm halfway through watching video clips."

"Don't argue about it, just do as you're told right away!" She takes him by the shoulder and pushes him toward the door.

" 'Oh, now we see the violence inherent in the system!' " he grumbles, ducking under her hand.

"Stop quoting Monty Python at me and go and feed the goats!" Chris shouts.

" 'Help, help, I'm being repressed!' " he shouts back as he goes through the door. A moment later he puts his head back in again. "Come on, Vick, you come too. I'll show you what to do and then you can take over. You're the one that loves animals so much."

41 THE ANIMALS are fed and Brenton and Victoria are walking back across the yard when they see the dust of a vehicle coming up the drive between the paddocks. The dust gleams white and opaque in the evening sun, contrasting sharply with the long, black shadows.

"That's Dad," Brenton remarks. "He's been out on the boat all day. Do you like sailing, Vicky?"

"I liked it when we were here before—when we used to go out in the little dinghy."

"Yeah, that was good fun! I used to like that too. We haven't got the dinghy anymore. Mum didn't want me to tell you yesterday . . ."

"I know about it," Vicky says. "Mick told me. The two boys were drowned. What a terrible thing to happen, wasn't it?"

Brenton doesn't tell her the most terrible thing, the thing he has never told anyone, that the boys had asked him to go with them, but he had looked at them, had imagined spending the afternoon in their company and had refused. But if he had gone with them, he would have known about the weather and . . .

"A lot of terrible things happen to people we know. Two boys from school were killed in a car accident at the end of last term. You should have seen the death notices in the paper—they got dozens and dozens." He screws up his eyes, frowning, for this is something that still puzzles him. "And they all said things like 'Rage on, mate' and 'God only takes the best,' as if they'd done something brilliant in getting themselves killed, as if they'd won some sort of competition."

He laughs as he says it, but Victoria is aware of the real anxiety behind the words. She desperately tries to think of something to say that will change the subject.

"Do you go out with your dad on the big boat?"

"I've been a couple of times. But the last time I got terribly seasick, and he hasn't wanted to take me since."

The seasickness attacked him out of the blue. He had never felt it before. It came after the loss of the dinghy, and it was something to do with the nightmares he had had of the cold, green unforgiving water closing over the heads of the two boys. Now he watches his father getting out of the Commodore, and he feels the customary flick of self-contempt he always gets when he sees himself through his father's eyes. Brenton sighs. "Let's go, Vicky, it must be time to eat."

42 VICTORIA has washed her hands and stands in the doorway looking at the room that used to be Brenton's and is now Brenton's and Michael's. The windows look out onto the wide, shady veranda, and the vines that cover the side of the house give it a greenish light. Chris has decorated the room in bright, clear blues and greens echoing the colors from outside. The floor is bare, polished wood with a dark-blue Spanish-style rug on it. On the walls are two huge posters of rock musicians, one group called Icehouse, the other Midnight Oil. Victoria has heard of the second, favorites of her father, but 63 not the first. Along the wall above Brenton's bed is his nuclear weapon collection.

Following her out of the bathroom, Brenton tells her, "You can go in if you want to. You can look at them close up."

Crossing the room she looks at the pictures and the lists of what should be inconceivable facts and figures. She knows all about them already, but she still cannot take them in. Her mind refuses to think about them.

"Doesn't it depress you having them there all the time?" Her hand goes up to her neck and she feels the cold beads.

Brenton doesn't reply. He is watching her face, wondering if she is going to be an ally, a friendly or a hostile element, on his side or on the side of the rest of the world.

The room is extremely tidy except for the area where Mick is now encamped.

"What a mess!" Victoria observes. His unmade bed is almost obliterated by an assortment of clothes and fishing gear.

"That's one of the reasons I hate sharing with Mick," Brenton complains with feeling. "He's so untidy and he messes all my things up."

"I'm sorry," Victoria apologizes. "It's all my fault. It must be an awful drag for you. Having me here, I mean."

"Oh well, I suppose we just have to get used to it. It's too far to send you home, isn't it? At least you won't be here in term time," Brenton replies, trying to sound jokey and friendly but not quite succeeding.

"Hurry up, kids!" Chris calls from the kitchen. "How long does it take you to wash your hands for heaven's sake? Are you having a bath or something?"

Victoria follows Brenton to the table feeling unwanted **64** and uncomfortable.

"SOME bloody lunatic from the city!"
Geoff Trethewan is saying as they sit down.

"Brenton thought it was rather artistic," Michael puts in, helping himself to lasagna.

The lasagna looks artistic, Victoria thinks, but then everything in Chris Trethewan's house does. The table, set for Sunday evening, looks like a magazine photograph—the peasantlike earthenware dish that holds the perfectly browned lasagna, the sea-green chunky tumblers, the homemade plaited bread that Geoff has just torn a piece off as though it is ordinary bread and not a work of art. How does she manage, Vicky wonders, to do so many different things?

"Just the sort of bloody stupid thing Brenton would say," Geoff explodes, almost choking on his bread. "Artistic! It's vandalism, plain and simple. These idiots come down from the city and think they can get away with that sort of thing here. If I catch them at it, I'll crucify them!"

"Crucify who?" Shelley slips gracefully into her seat. Her eyes are bright and happy and a wonderful smell of bath salts, talcum powder and perfume hangs around her.

"The phantom graffiti artist," Brenton informs her. "The one that decorated the hospital." He takes a quick look at his father and amends his sentence. "I mean the phantom graffiti *vandal* who *defaced* the hospital." He emphasizes the words carefully and gives his father a wide and infuriating grin.

"Jason said he'd throw them off the jetty," Shelley re- **65** marks, inspecting the lasagna critically. "Can I have just salad, Mum? This stuff is terribly fattening!"

"One!" counts Michael.

"Shut up!" she says and kicks him under the table.

"We count how often she mentions his name every meal," Michael explains to Victoria. "Her record is twenty-five times during the course of one meal."

"Jason's got a damn sight more sense than either of you two," their father observes scornfully.

"Oh, I'd throw them off the jetty too," Michael assures him quickly. "It's only Brenton who . . ."

"That's enough, Michael," his mother interrupts sharply. "Let's drop the subject. Get on with your meal."

"I've nearly finished," he tells her, injured.

"I can't think how. You've hardly stopped talking since you sat down!"

"I can eat while I talk," he boasts, demonstrating.

"Mum," Shelley pleads. "Tell him not to be so gross. Whatever will Vicky think of us?"

"She's one of the family now." Chris looks across the table at Victoria and smiles at her with her eyes. "I suppose she'll just have to get used to us."

They are exaggerating their normal ways of interacting for her benefit. She is the audience and they are the actors.

Victoria's presence is having a certain effect on the whole family, altering it in slight and subtle ways. They are showing off to her, letting her see what a lively and interesting family they are, showing the side they like to present in public. She smiles back at Chris and wonders if she will ever be unselfconsciously one of them and no longer an outsider.

Playing the part of a dutiful daughter, Shelley inquires, **66** "How'd you go on the boat, Dad?"

"Not bad. We would have come third overall, but I ducked out of the last event—it would have meant getting home too late and Mum wanted me to be here, seeing as it's Vicky's first weekend." He smiles kindly at her.

"I wouldn't have minded," she says, thinking the more they try to make her feel at home the less at home she feels.

"I'll take you out with me one day. Would you like that?" When she nods he goes on, "You don't get seasick, do you?"

"I don't know. I don't think so."

"Brenton does," Mick says innocently.

Geoff laughs. "I'll say. Last time he came out we thought he was going to chuck up his guts!"

"Not at mealtime, dear," Chris remonstrates.

"It wasn't my fault," Brenton adds. Michael however wants to tell the whole story. "Dad took him racing. It was meant to be a super-special treat but Brenton was so sick they had to pull out of the race. They were in the lead too!"

"I didn't do it on purpose!" Something in Brenton's voice warns Victoria that he is starting to rise to the needling that has been going on since the meal began. She hopes the subject will be allowed to drop but sees that Michael does not intend to drop it.

"And then, when they got back to shore, Brenton couldn't even walk. Dad had to carry him off the boat. And he threw up one last time, all over Dad . . ." He is going to tell more, but Brenton now goes into attack.

"Shut up!" he shouts. "Shut your bloody mouth or I'll shut it for you!" He pushes back his chair and jumps to his feet. In doing so his arm catches the water jug and sends it sideways across the table. The water streams coldly and inevitably into his father's lap. Geoff leaps to his feet too.

"For God's sake!" he says disgustedly, brushing the water **67** ineffectually off his trousers. "Can't you control your temper? Isn't it ever possible to have a meal in peace in this place?"

Michael surveys the damage with wide eyes. "Sorry! It was only a joke. I was just telling Vicky what happened."

"Get a cloth and wipe the table, Brenton," Chris orders icily. "Then sit down and try not to overreact."

"It was Mick's fault," he replies angrily. "He started it all. He always does. And you always blame me."

"You don't have to fly off the handle at every little thing."

"Brenton always does," Shelley comments from the sidelines.

"You stay out of it, Shelley!"

"You see," she explains. "He always escalates everything. You can just be having an ordinary family argument, nothing specially bad, and Brenton turns it into a major confrontation. You're so keen on world peace," she challenges him. "Why don't we have a little world peace around here? It's like charity, it begins at home."

A rather stormy silence follows this unanswerable logic. Brenton tosses the wet cloth back into the sink and sits down. His father returns in dry trousers, but still scowling.

Chris says, in an effort to break the atmosphere, "I read something funny like that in a book the other day. There was this young fellow who joined the communist party, and his mother said to him, 'Now you're a communist, do you think you could help with the housework?' "

Her three children stare blankly at her. No one laughs.

"That's the sort of thing that only a mother would find funny," Brenton mutters.

Shelley also makes an effort to lighten things. "That's a pretty necklace, Vicky. Did you get it in Nigeria?"

As Victoria shakes her head she catches Michael's eye.

68 He is giving her a telling look.

"Where did you get it?" Shelley persists. "I've never seen one so pretty. I'd love to have one."

"Somebody gave it to me," Victoria replies evasively. She is wishing she had not worn the necklace now, afraid that Shelley's questioning will force her to reveal that she got it from a complete stranger on the beach. Doubtless the Trethewan parents, just like her own, don't approve of accepting presents from strangers, and they will tell her she must take it back.

"Pass your plate to me," Chris says, interrupting her thoughts, "and I'll get dessert."

Shelley stands up to help her mother clear the table, and as she comes behind Vicky she reaches out and takes hold of the necklace. "What a lovely feel it's got," she exclaims.

"It *is* lovely," Chris agrees. "I've never seen anything like it before. What are the beads made of, Vicky?"

"I don't know," she admits. "Some sort of plastic, I suppose."

Chris reaches out and feels the necklace. "Goodness, isn't it cold!"

"I wish you could get me one for Christmas," Shelley says as she takes the plates over to the sink. "It feels so lovely." She turns back to the table. "What's for dessert, Mum?"

"There's strawberry shortcake and ice cream in the freezer." When Shelley groans in despair, Chris goes on, "There's some unfattening fruit salad too—you can have some of that!"

Shelley puts all three desserts on the table. "Vicky, I couldn't just borrow it for tonight, could I? I'd love to show it to Jason. I'd be ever so careful with it."

Vicky hesitates. If it were a normal necklace she wouldn't mind at all, but she doesn't want to let this particular one out of her sight. Luckily, Brenton comes to the rescue. **69**

"Of course you can't borrow it, Shell. It's Vicky's. It might be valuable. The poor girl hasn't been in the house for twenty-four hours and you're already stealing her things. You have to watch Shelley," he says warningly to Victoria. "She's got no principles at all!"

"I wouldn't mind usually," Vicky replies. "It's just that this necklace is rather special."

She takes a mouthful of strawberry shortcake and lays down her fork.

"Don't you like it?" Chris inquires.

"It's delicious," she replies, truthfully. "It's just that I'm not very hungry."

"What's the food like where you've been living?" Michael asks, finding this a far more interesting subject than the necklace. "Do you eat normal food like us?"

"They eat goats," Brenton informs him.

"Goats! Yuck!"

"Don't be silly," Chris scolds. "Goat meat is just like lamb, isn't it Vicky? You're all perfectly happy to eat that."

"I don't really like eating goats," Vicky says slowly. "But sometimes that's all there is to eat. Lawrence, our cook, makes kebabs out of them, and stews and so on. And we eat chickens quite often, and there's a wonderful thing called peanut stew—you have lots and lots of little side dishes with it."

"Your cook? Do you have servants?" Michael cannot believe it. "You lucky thing! I suppose you never have to do any washing up! I thought you were meant to be poor," he adds ingenuously.

"Everybody has servants there," Vicky explains to him. "Actually Mum and Dad don't particularly like it. They hate having to tell other people what to do and Mum says **70** she would rather do her own housework. But everyone has servants—you more or less have to—and it means we're giving work to a whole family. They're like part of our family, really. Simon and I help them. It's fun. They teach us Hausa—that's the local language—and Yoruba, their language—and we play with their children."

She has a sudden vivid image of that African kitchen. It seems like somewhere light-years away. She can see Lawrence in his white shirt and trousers standing gravely by the cooker, Lavinia in her bright patterned cotton skirt washing vegetables at the sink and outside on the step the clutch of little children, with their liquid eyes and smooth, beautifully shaped heads. She can smell the curious mixture of insecticide, butane gas and peanuts, mingled with the rich earth smell of Africa. A pang of homesickness shoots through her, so sharp it nearly brings tears to her eyes. She gazes at this other kitchen and the family at whose table she now sits.

"Everything's so different here." She sounds almost helpless.

"You'll soon get used to it," Chris assures her comfortingly.

"I suppose I will." But secretly Victoria is not sure she wants to.

44

THE MEAL is over. Shelley has disappeared to spend the evening with Jason; Brenton and his father are watching television in uneasy silence; Chris has retreated to her sewing room; Michael, having conceded with intense protest that it might be his turn, is doing the washing up.

"You help me, Vicky. Washing up is fun for you because you haven't had to do it for two years."

She looks out of the window. It is still light, but it will not be for much longer. "I said I'd go back and see that boy. Do you think I should?"

"I couldn't tell you before," Michael replies. "I saw him. I went back while you were asleep."

"You did? Was he still there? What did you think of him?"

"You didn't tell me he was black," Michael complains, as though that somehow made a big difference to the situation. "And I think he's a bit of a con artist. He took my Walkman off me." He pauses while he scrubs at a plate with extreme vigor and slings it haphazardly in the general direction of the rack. Victoria rescues it and dries it carefully.

"You mean he pinched it from you?"

"Well, not exactly." Michael sounds aggrieved and puzzled. "I gave it to him, but I didn't really mean to, and now I wish I hadn't. He's probably taken off by now and I'll never see it again. Mum and Dad gave it to me for my birthday. They'll be really fed up if I lose it. I hate washing up this meal," he adds gloomily. "The water goes all orange from the sauce and it sticks to everything."

"But did you think there was anything strange about him?"

"Oh, I don't know! He's definitely a bit weird . . . but a lot of Abos are."

Victoria doesn't know how to react to this comment. She never thought the strange boy was an Aboriginal despite his dark skin; she hates the word Abo, and she doesn't like the sweeping generalization. She realizes how much being so close to her parents' work in Nigeria has changed her. Suddenly she feels years older than Michael. She looks at him with something close to dislike and says, "What about the necklace?"

Michael laughs as he tackles the saucepans. "Wasn't that funny at dinner? Shelley really put you on the spot." Then he grows more serious. "I don't think it was a very good idea to take it from him," he tells her. "Perhaps you should give it back?"

"Did he give you anything?"

"Just a bit of old junk. He probably picked it up at the dump." Michael places the last saucepan in the rack and pulls the plug out of the sink. The water rushes away with a whoosh and a gurgle, leaving a greasy orange rim. "You clean out the sink," he suggests, "and I'll put the things away. You won't know where they go."

"All right," Vicky agrees, drying up the final saucepan and placing it next to all the other utensils on the bench top. "Let's see the piece of junk, though."

She turns on the hot tap, squirts detergent in the sink and attacks the grease with the scrubbing brush.

Michael watches her in amazement. "You look as though you're really enjoying it."

"I am quite. It's rather good fun splashing the water around."

"As a special treat you can do it every day of the holidays," he promises her. He stows the saucepans hurriedly into the cupboard and shuts the door firmly before they can all fall out again.

"We'll go down and find him in the morning," he says, "and get the Walkman back." Then he takes something out of his pocket and shows it to her. It is a metal disk about the size of a jam-jar lid, with a reflecting sheen like a very dark mirror. Victoria looks at it as it lies in Michael's palm. **73**

Then she dries the soapy water off her hands and takes it gently. It feels like a perfectly ordinary piece of metal. She turns it over. "I wonder what it's for."

"It's just a piece of junk," Michael says again.

"Perhaps it's some kind of mirror," Victoria says, peering into it. She can dimly see her face, and then she has the impression that, if only she could concentrate hard enough, she would be able to see something else in it . . . something obscure, yet familiar, like her own mind. . . . She looks up with a shiver, and hands the disk back to Michael, who puts it away in his pocket without looking at it. Beads and mirrors, she is thinking. Little trinkets that he thinks will appeal to them. Gifts for the natives.

"That's what they are," she says out loud. "Beads and mirrors for the natives."

Michael is already halfway out the door so there is no one in the kitchen to hear. Victoria is all alone with the logical conclusion. The boy on the beach is not human. He has come from somewhere else. He is an alien.

She knows it must be true and yet she can't believe it. Most of the night the suspicion keeps returning to her and she pushes it away. Again it is nearly dawn before she sleeps.

45 AT BREAKFAST the next morning Chris announces, "I'm going in to Willstown to do some shopping. Does anyone want to come?"

Michael and Victoria exchange looks. "What time?" Michael asks. "We've got something to do first."

"In about an hour. Will you be ready then? When we've
74 tidied the house and done the washing up."

"Brenton's turn," Mick declares, pushing back his chair and getting up from the table in a hurry. "Don't go without us!"

As they run out the door Brenton is complaining, "I think it's Shelley's turn."

"You'd better come too," his mother tells him. "I don't suppose you've done any Christmas shopping yet, have you?"

"I think I might duck out of Christmas this year!"

"Don't be silly!" Chris is not sure if it is a joke or not. "You can't duck out of Christmas. You always enjoy it anyway!"

"You want everyone to enjoy it," he points out, "because it's your great production. Brilliant food, brilliant decorations, brilliant family life . . . you more or less force everyone to enjoy it. And all that happens is that Dad drinks too much, and nobody really likes their presents and it all costs too much money and you end up crying."

He looks moodily out of the window as the sink fills up with water. The lavender haze is there again. Of course, he thinks, it's nothing to do with French nuclear testing. You can't see radioactive fallout. It's just general pollution from the city over the horizon. Still, it reminds him of another aspect of Christmas that gets up his nose. "Peace and goodwill to all men," he says disgustedly. "What a bloody lie!"

Chris opens the cupboard door and all the saucepans cascade out onto the floor.

"For heaven's sake!" she exclaims. "Who put them all away like that? Was that you, Brenton?"

"No it was not!" he replies, outraged. "See how you always blame me for everything? The dear little bunnies, Micky and Vicky, did the washing up last night, remember?"

"Oh, so they did," she admits, putting the saucepans away neatly, but she is still irritated with him and she does not apologize.

46

BRENTON has made his bed and he now sits on it, looking distastefully at Michael's unmade bed and throwing the dice from one hand to the other. If he's going to duck out of Christmas there's the question of presents. To buy or not to buy, he says dreamily to himself, that is the question. It's an alarming decision, one that will set him at odds with the whole family and cause some unpleasant waves, he has no doubt about that. He gives himself favorable odds: ten or over not to buy, nine or under, to buy.

Whistling softly he throws the dice down on the quilt.

Outside, the car horn toots impatiently.

Double six. Unequivocal. He starts to laugh. A mad feeling of freedom races through him. He picks up the dice, puts them in his pocket and runs out of the room.

He jumps into the front seat next to his mother and gives her a grin of satisfaction. He has cut one more of the ties that bind him through his family to a hypocritical society. He is marginally more free.

47 VICTORIA and Michael are peering warily over the wall alongside the shack. The 4WD is not there and the place appears deserted, apart from the rottweiler, which is lying on the porch, nose on paws, watching them with one eye.

"Gone out," Michael hisses. "Reckon we can risk it."

As they clamber over the wall and skirt the cottage, the dog leaps to its feet and barks at them frantically. They ignore it and make for the beach.

The sea is receding sluggishly toward the horizon, creeping away inch by inch, reluctantly obeying the unseen moon. Where it has been secretly at night the sand is wet and squelchy, alive with crabs, smelling of seaweed and slime.

"I bet he's not there anymore," Michael pants. "I bet I never see my Walkman again."

Victoria doesn't answer, but privately she agrees with him. The beach seems its ordinary, everyday self. How could anything so extraordinary happen on it? She is rather surprised that she should have imagined something so unlikely. Surely she has grown beyond having the weird and fantastic ideas she had when she was younger and has become more down-to-earth and dependable. It makes her feel as though she does not know herself, as though she has suddenly become someone unrecognizable.

As they round the headland, beach, cliffs and caves all seem equally empty, apart from the pigeons that wheel and turn above their nesting places, their feathers gleaming in the early morning sun.

Michael swears viciously, but quite unselfconsciously. It surprises Victoria. She giggles to hide the fact, but also from nervousness. She's worried about the radio too now, feeling that if it is lost it will be her fault.

Just as she is thinking that no one is there, she realizes with shock that someone is. A tiny movement flickers against the rocks, and when she screws up her eyes she can see a small round dark patch that is not a hole in the cliff, but someone's face.

"He's there!" Michael exclaims in relief. "Come on!"

They begin to run. Now she can see a distinct figure, its arm raised in welcome.

Above their heads a cloud of pigeons takes off in alarm, circles over the retreating sea and settles again.

48 HE LOOKS the same as the day before—thin, dark-skinned, with black eyes and a shock of brown hair that stands out around his head like a chrysanthemum. The camouflage clothes are the same. He gives them the same close, intent scrutiny and holds himself in the same tense, slightly nervous way. But this time he speaks in English.

"Good morning!" he says in a voice that is too deep and too old for his size and his face.

Neither of them says anything. They stand and stare, their mouths open.

The strange boy gestures at the sky. "Weather on the gulf will be fine and warm," he declares. "Winds five to ten
78 knots with a slight swell."

When they do not respond to this piece of information he looks at them and frowns. He is holding the radio in his hand, but he does not offer to return it to Michael. Instead he speaks again, more hesitantly, as though he is listening to someone piecing together the words, rather than repeating phrases he has learned by heart.

"Thanks for the radio." His voice is still deep and adult. "I used it to . . ." He pauses as though he cannot quite hear the next word and smiles. "It is not there yet," he explains, holding up the silver object in his other hand. It is smooth and rectangular, rather like an outsize plastic card. "The language machine can only record words. It cannot make them up from nothing. That is, sometimes it can make them up following patterns. But your language is hard; the patterns are not clear."

Since this speech means very little to Victoria and Michael they still don't speak. There is another long pause. The boy says hopefully, "All hits all the time?"

Michael begins to giggle with nervousness. Victoria says slowly, "Your voice is too deep. Only men speak like that. You should speak like Michael, like this boy." She gives Michael a push. "Say something to him, Mick!"

Michael swallows with a gulp. For once in his life he is totally speechless.

"What are men?" the stranger inquires.

It's easier answering a question, but not much. Michael says, "Adults, grown-ups, you know, big people."

"Men are bigger than me?"

Michael looks at him. He is about the same size as Brenton, a shade shorter than Michael himself.

"Yeah, a lot bigger than you."

The black eyes widen with a touch of apprehension. The boy asks, "You are not men? What are you?" His voice has **79** gone up in pitch. He is sounding more like a teenager and less like a thirty-year-old.

"We are children," Victoria says. "Kids. When we grow up we become men. At least boys," she points to Michael, "become men, and girls like me grow up to be women."

"Women," he repeats, holds up the silvery card and looks at it. The information seems to interest him considerably. Then he turns back to the children and says, "I am fully grown up. Therefore I am an adult."

Michael snorts in disbelief. "You're a nut case, mate!"

Victoria shakes his arm. "Don't," she says. "Let's listen to him. We can find out who he is."

"He's a raving lunatic, that's who he is." Michael scoffs. "Give me back my radio," he demands.

The dark boy says casually, "I will keep it a little longer. It is still useful to me."

When Michael opens his mouth to protest he receives a look that silences him. It suddenly seems important not to argue. It's an unfamiliar feeling to him; while he is wrestling with it, Cal speaks to Vicky.

"Your name is Vicky. What is his?"

"Michael," she says, and adds, "he's sometimes called Mick or Micky."

"Vicky and Micky," the boy repeats, smiling at how they rhyme. Then he resumes his studious face and asks, "Do these names mean anything?"

"Vicky is short for Victoria and that means victorious." When he looks blank she explains. "Like a winner. And Michael means Prince of God."

"It does not!" Michael interrupts hotly. "It's got nothing to do with God."

"Yes it has," she insists. "It's in the Bible."

80   Michael is tired of this, to him, crazy conversation. He

feels uncomfortable and uneasy. He can't believe this peculiar fellow next to him is anything unearthly, and that means he has to be mad, and he's not only mad, he's also black. "Come on, Vicky," he urges irritably. "Mum'll crack up if we keep her waiting."

Cal notices the anger. "Wait here a minute," he says. "I will give you another present."

He goes back to the cave and returns with a small pack. Pulling it apart, he takes from inside it a necklace like Victoria's. "For you!" he says, and gives it to Michael.

"I don't want a dumb necklace," Michael explodes. "That's for girls!" He steps back and refuses to take it.

"Ah, for girls," Cal observes, nodding several times. "How fascinating! I have made him angry," he says to Vicky. "I am sorry."

"He's just being stupid," she says. "Don't bother about him." She reaches out and feels the material of the pack. It is a lot less flimsy than it looks, and when she tries to pull the pack apart, she can't.

"It is mine; it only opens for me," Cal says, as though having to explain something self-evident. He demonstrates, and Victoria sees inside another disklike object, larger than the one Michael brought home but made of the same dully gleaming metal. "What's that?" she says curiously.

Cal brings it out and shows it to her. "This is my life-support system." He points to the sun. "It helps me convert sunlight to feed me and keeps me in touch."

In touch with whom? Vicky wants to ask, but Michael interrupts sourly. "I suppose he's some sort of plant!" He is getting more and more agitated. It is not only that he is afraid they are going to be late, there is something about this stranger carrying on as though he is so superior to Michael and Vicky, as though he is somehow infinitely *81* more civilized and Michael is some sort of native! The realization outrages him.

"Yes, you're right," Vicky agrees, too fascinated by Cal to notice Michael's reaction. "Like a plant. It must be a sort of photosynthesis."

Michael gives her an incredulous look. "What are you talking about? And since when are you so up on technology?"

"It's something Dad told me about—you know he's a geneticist? One day we'll all be able to live on sunlight. . . . Something about getting the right genes from plants."

"That's just science fiction!" Michael shakes his head. "I'll be back later," he warns Cal. "And if you don't give me the radio then you'll be in real trouble!"

Without waiting for Victoria he turns and heads off over the rocks.

"Micky," she calls after him. "Come back! Don't you realize. . . ?" Her heart is beating so strongly it almost chokes her, and she is trembling with excitement. She knows what she suspected last night is completely and unmistakably true. The figure standing before her is an alien . . . an extraterrestrial . . . a spaceman. . . . But none of the science-fiction words seem to fit this slight, dark person, who has a name, Cal, and who is now reaching out and gesturing at her clothes.

"Bring me some of these," Cal says.

"Vicky!" Michael's distant voice is angry.

"I'd better go," Victoria says. "I'll come back later. I'll bring you some clothes if I can."

"Then you can show me where you live. I would like to see some men."

Gee, Victoria is thinking, that might be a little difficult. All the same she finds herself saying "OK" again.

He smiles at her and nods his head several times as though to encourage and reassure her. "I will not hurt you. Don't be afraid of me."

She is not afraid. On the contrary, she is feeling rather sorry for him, whoever he might be, so far away from his own world, an alien. She wants to reassure him. She puts out her hand and touches the brown skin, just above his wrist. She feels him tense up and flinch, as if in revulsion. She lets go with a sigh. "Good-bye," she says.

"Good-bye," he repeats, and dismisses her with a nod. He puts the earphones on his head and begins to fiddle with the tuning button. Victoria jumps nimbly over the rocks and down onto the sand where she can run. When she looks back Cal has disappeared.

49 FROM the top of the cliff Victoria can hear the car horn honking impatiently. The rottweiler barks again futilely as she climbs the wall. The car is waiting in the road outside the shack fence and Michael is already in it.

"What on earth were you doing?" Brenton demands. "We've been waiting for ages."

"Sorry," Victoria apologizes. Michael says nothing. He does not look at Vicky. He is scowling out the window. Chris observes them both in the rearview mirror. They are sitting on opposite sides of the backseat, as far away from each other as possible, with the self-justifying look of children who have just quarreled. She sighs in disquiet, hoping they are not going to squabble all through the holidays.

"Where do you want to go?" she inquires.

"I'm going to Rawlings'," Michael answers.

"Brenton?"

"Nowhere in particular," he responds. "I've decided not to buy any presents this year, so it doesn't matter really." He turns to his mother as he says it and bestows a triumphant smile on her.

"Come on, Brenton," she says in exasperation. "You've got to buy people presents. It's Christmas."

"Well, I've decided not to," he says casually.

"Does that mean we don't have to buy you anything?" Michael demands.

"Sure," Brenton replies. "Nobody need buy me anything. I'll buy whatever I want with the money I would have spent on you—much less hassle for everyone."

His mother doesn't say anything, but her lips tighten and she drives a little faster.

50 ALMOST before the car has stopped outside the supermarket in Willstown, Michael has jumped out and escaped down the street. His mother stares after him in annoyance as she puts the handbrake on.

"Brenton, can you look after Vicky? She'll be terribly bored if she has to tag along after me."

"I suppose so," he says without a great deal of enthusiasm. "Come on, Vicky."

She follows him rather mutinously, not used to having to trail along after people who don't want her to be with them, feeling like a parcel on legs. She's glad she has a secret that Brenton knows nothing about. It gives her a feeling of satisfaction as she walks down the street behind him. Cal is going to be her own friend; she will keep him to herself.

"Where are we going, Brenton?" she demands, catching up with him.

"Rawlings', I guess. Nowhere else much to go."

51 RAWLINGS' is a general store selling everything from curiously old-fashioned looking clothes to amazingly modern diving equipment. Michael is already inside, inspecting the fishing gear with his two best mates, Danny and Craig, who, like him, are rather large, fair-haired and blue-eyed. They look up when the doorbell rings, to see Brenton slipping into the store, shoulders hunched and hands in pockets, followed by Victoria.

"Here's your brother!"

"Hey, Brenton, who's your girlfriend?" Craig whispers something to Danny, and all three boys fall about laughing.

Acting as though they are on another planet, Brenton walks over to inspect the diving equipment. Vicky finds herself abandoned in the entrance to the shop. There's a moment when she is starting to walk over to join Michael, but he looks at her as though he has never seen her before in his life and turns his back. He whispers something to Craig and Danny and again the ugly, unfunny laughter erupts in the shop.

Convinced they are laughing at her, Vicky's face goes hot and her skin prickles under her shirt collar. She turns **85** abruptly and studies the display of shells in the window with desperately assumed interest. Among the huge shining cowries and turban shells is the entire jaw of a large fish, its needle-sharp teeth perfectly preserved. It reminds her of her brother, Simon. It is just the sort of thing he loves.

She wishes passionately he were now with her, forgetting how much they used to squabble and how irritating he can be. He is a million times better than the two Trethewan boys, she thinks, feeling betrayed and angry, and also slightly desperate. How is she going to survive with this family? She's got to spend the next seven weeks with them. She can't escape from them; there's nowhere else to go. Her eyes have started to water dangerously. She blinks them rapidly and tries to think of something else, but the boys' voices intrude again, echoing through the store with exaggerated loudness.

"Oh how gay!"

"You really turn me on, Brenton!"

Brenton is trying on a diving mask. Its black oval eclipses his thin face. Ignoring the teasing he puts it back and tries on another.

"It's the monster from the freaking deep!"

"It's the faggot from the freaking deep!"

 THE DOORBELL rings. Looking up from her scrutiny of the shells Vicky sees Brenton disappear down the street.

"Hey, Brenton!" the boys yell after him. "You forgot your

freaking girlfriend!"

"She freaking scared him off!"

"He wouldn't freaking know what to do with her!"

They walk out of the stop jostling each other, laughing and swearing. Victoria watches them go with loathing in her heart. She feels betrayed by Michael and, though she doesn't want to admit it, offended by the boys' language. Her life has been the opposite of sheltered; she has seen poverty, disease and death firsthand, but the people among whom she has seen them are reserved and dignified. Even the most deprived of them do not drop obscenities around the way these golden-haired boys do, so lightly and so casually.

I suppose I'll get used to it, she thinks.

But again she finds herself wondering how much she wants to become a part of this life and how much she wants to remain herself. She has a momentary flash of her father's face, thin and tanned, his hair going slightly gray, his eyes bright and cheerful behind his glasses. If he were here he would know what to do. He would say something to the boys that was both jokey and sensible, disarming them, defusing the situation and leaving everyone feeling OK.

But Victoria is all alone. She has to handle everything herself even though she is sure she is going to make a mess of it.

When she comes out of the shop she thinks she already has. There is no sign of either Brenton or Michael, and she has forgotten the way back to the car.

53 "HOW COULD you lose her?" Chris Trethewan demands furiously. "Didn't you realize she doesn't know her way around?"

"I didn't lose her," Brenton explains patiently. "I left her in Rawlings'. Mick was there," he adds, giving his brother a loaded look. "Why didn't he look after her?"

"She came in with you, I thought she was going out with you. Anyway, there's no need to crack up—she can't get lost in Willstown. I'll go out on a search party. I'll find her!"

"Here she comes," Brenton says. He has spotted her dark head weaving its way rather erratically through the holiday crowds. He waves and shouts, "Hey, Vicky! Over here!"

Victoria looks in the direction of the shout, screwing up her eyes and squinting against the sun. She does not look very certain, but she starts to head toward where the Trethewans are standing by the Falcon.

"Gee, she's half blind, Mum," Michael comments. "She must need glasses."

"Perhaps I'd better get her eyes tested," Chris remarks. "It's rather a nuisance. It probably means a trip to the city."

"Sorry." Victoria has the feeling she is apologizing rather a lot lately. "I forgot which way the car was. I thought I remembered perfectly how to get around Willstown, but it all seems to have changed."

"It has changed since you were here," Chris says. "There's the new supermarket complex and many more shops."

"I can't imagine anyone getting lost in Willstown," Michael mutters scathingly.

"Brenton really should have looked after you better," Chris tells Victoria.

"Oh, Mum!" he butts in. "The sooner she finds her own way around the better. She's got to be one of the family. We can't baby-sit her all the time."

"I can find my own way around," Victoria answers hotly. "You don't have to look after me. I don't want to be any trouble to any of you!"

With an effort she keeps herself from adding, "So there!" but the unspoken words hang in the air just the same. The atmosphere in the car as they drive home is even more uncomfortable than on the journey out.

54 MICHAEL breaks the silence as they approach the Farborough turnoff. "Can you drop me at the pool, Mum? I said I'd meet Craig and Danny there."

"You'd better come home and have some lunch, hadn't you? And what about your swimsuit?"

"I've got it on. And I can get a pie at the kiosk."

Chris takes the right-hand turn to Farborough. The swimming pool is a saltwater one, built among the rocks of a small headland. Almost empty at low tide, it gradually fills with fresh, cool water as the tide comes in. The waves break over a sloping concrete wall that divides the pool from the sea, and a shark net across the mouth of the small inlet ensures that swimmers can venture fearlessly out into the deep water.

Since the previous summer it has been rebuilt and redecorated. As the Trethewans pull up in the car park above **89** the pool it is at once obvious that someone else has taken a hand in redecorating it even further. In swirls of green and orange paint across the cream walls of the kiosk and changing rooms, someone has written DEADEN DEADEN DEADEN.

"Wow!" Michael exclaims. "The phantom strikes again!"

"Didn't he have time to add the D?" Brenton wonders aloud. "Or did he mean to write deaden, this time, and not dead end?"

His mother, outraged, is not listening to him. "Well, really!" she says. "It's disgusting! All that work to get the place looking decent again, and all the money the council spent on it. Who is it that does this sort of thing?"

"I'll ask Danny!" Michael jumps out of the car, waving to one of the boys who was with him in Rawlings'. "He'll know all about it." Danny's parents own the general store in Penbowie, a clearinghouse of local gossip.

"How will you get back?" Chris calls after him.

"Someone will give me a lift, I expect. If not I'll phone Dad."

"Have you got zinc on your nose?"

"Yeah, Mum. See you!" He gives them a perfunctory wave and leaps down the steps.

"What about you two?" Chris asks. "Do either of you want to stay?"

It looks cool and inviting. Victoria would like to stay, but she doesn't want to spend the afternoon being ignored, or worse, by Mick and his friends. "I haven't got my suit," she says truthfully.

"Brenton?"

"No way!" Brenton looks as if he would rather die.

His mother sighs. "It's a shame you can't be like Michael," she observes, as she backs the Falcon out of the car park. "Brenton finds it rather hard to make friends," she explains to Victoria.

"I don't find it hard to make friends," he contradicts her. "It's just there's no one here to make friends with."

"Perhaps you're too fussy?" she suggests. The accusing note that comes when she is angry with the world in general and taking it out on him in particular is creeping back into her voice. He replies aggressively, "I'd rather have no friends at all than hang around with the jerks Mick likes."

Victoria stares out of the window at the flat, stark countryside. She is thinking that what Shelley said the previous night is true. Brenton does overreact. He does escalate every argument into a major confrontation. But at the same time it seems to her that they all pick on Brenton without really noticing it anymore. He has become the general scapegoat, and she can't help feeling a bit sorry for him.

She knows intuitively she is going to have to study this family and break their secret code of behavior, but she's still not sure she wants to be a part of them, and trying to follow their complex interaction is tiring her out. She yawns and closes her eyes, leaning her head back on the seat. The car has a hot, plastic smell that makes her feel slightly sick.

Chris is watching her in the mirror. "Tired, Vicky?"

She opens her eyes and meets the reflection. "Mmm" she nods.

"Sleep any better last night?"

"A bit." She does not elaborate, not wanting to explain that she had again lain wakeful and thirsty in the early hours of the morning, wondering what she was doing in this alien place among strangers, finally crying into her pillow, making her throat ache until she fell asleep again.

"You'd better have a rest this afternoon," Chris suggests. **91**

"You can go swimming later. I can run you up to the pool, or you can go down to the beach when the tide's in."

"Yes, I'll go down to the beach." Vicky has remembered that she said she would take Cal some clothes. She wonders how she will get hold of them. She looks at Brenton, sitting in the front seat wrapped in his own personal cloud of anger. I suppose I could ask him, she thinks.

55 "WILL YOU give me a hand with the washing, Vicky?" Chris asks when they have finished the dishes from lunch and tidied the kitchen.

The clean clothes smell beautifully of a mixture of sea air and lemon as Vicky takes them off the line and folds them. Chris is moving the sprinklers on the flowerbeds around the house. She smiles as Vicky presses the towels up against her face and sniffs them.

"Come over here and smell these!"

Victoria puts the last piece of clothing into the laundry basket and crosses the grass. Chris holds out a sprig to her.

"It smells just like the clothes," Vicky exclaims.

"It's lemon thyme," Chris tells her. "This is my herb garden. Try this one. It's rosemary."

The heady perfume clings to Vicky's fingers and follows her as she moves around the garden.

"The herbs like growing by the sea," Chris remarks. "The air seems to suit them."

"Your garden is so pretty," Vicky replies. "But everywhere else," she makes a gesture at the surrounding countryside, **92** "is so bare."

"It looks barren," Chris agrees. "But it's surprisingly good farming country, when it gets enough rain. Still, I sometimes wish they'd left a bit of scrub when the land was cleared. I often wonder what it looked like before the Europeans came." She changes the subject. "Look at Tang, Vicky!"

The Burmese cat is stealthily creeping up on the hose as the water begins to trickle through it. He pounces on it and gives it a sharp jab with his paw. At the same moment jets of water begin to shoot from the sprinkler. The cat leaps back, shaking drops from his head, his face outraged. He gives the woman and the girl a reproachful look and walks away in dignity to lie in a cool spot under the lavender. It is no accident that the mauve and gray tones of the bush contrast perfectly with his velvet-brown fur.

"Poor Tang!" Vicky laughs.

"He can't resist playing with it," Chris says. "And it always catches him out. Doesn't he look beautiful under the lavender, Vicky? He always chooses somewhere to sit that suits his coloring."

She picks up the laundry basket and walks toward the house. "Do you want to get a book and have a rest? There's a stack of books in the boys' room if you'd like to borrow something. I'm going to make some Christmas decorations. We'll put up the tree tonight. That reminds me, I haven't made my mince pies yet. And I've got to finish the new dress I'm making Shelley for Christmas."

She smiles ruefully and almost apologetically at Victoria. "I'm sorry I can't entertain you more, but there's always so much to do."

Victoria holds open the screen door so Chris can get inside with the basket of clean clothes. "That's OK," she says. "I'm quite happy entertaining myself." **93**

56 "CAN I borrow a book?"

Brenton looks up from his bed where he is sitting, dice in hand, having been away for a good half hour in the *Labyrinth of Dead Ends*. He considers Vicky's request, wondering if it's worth taking a gamble on, deciding it's not.

"I suppose so," he says and returns to the *Labyrinth*.

Victoria studies the books. They are a strange assortment, reflecting the entire childhood of the three Trethewan children, and ranging from Dr. Seuss to science fiction. There is also a large number of game books. She takes one of these down and opens it. It does not look very restful. She thinks her own life already contains too many difficult choices. She puts it back on the shelf and gazes over at Brenton.

He throws the dice, turns the pages of the book and makes a note on a piece of paper. Then he sighs, looks out of the window, throws the dice, turns to another page.

"Oh damn!" he exclaims and closes the book with a snap.

"What are you doing? What's the matter?"

"I drank something I thought was a nourishing potion and it turned out to be deadly poison."

"Huh?"

He holds up the book and shows it to her. "It's a game book. I'm trying to find my way through the Labyrinth, but I keep running into dead ends. Story of my life," he adds gloomily.

"If I ask you for something, will you say yes or no, without **94** asking what for?" Victoria finds herself saying.

He frowns at her. "That depends," he answers, rolling the dice from one hand to the other.

"What on?"

"On my little friends here. Let's say, six and under, they're telling me to help you, over six they're telling me not to." He throws the dice. Six and three fall uppermost.

"Sorry!" Brenton says, picking them up and smiling at Victoria.

She stares back at him, baffled and frustrated. Then she takes a book at random off the shelf and walks out of the room.

57

SHE LIES on her bed and opens the book. It is called *Safari Adventure*, and she thinks she might enjoy it because it is set in Africa, but it turns out to be nothing like the Africa she knows, and after a few pages she lets it fall on the bed. She is drifting into sleep and thinking she really mustn't let herself, when there is a knock on the door. It opens and Brenton comes into the room.

"I've decided I was wrong," he announces. "It wasn't fair to throw the dice on your question."

"It wasn't?" she replies, wondering what he is talking about.

"No, because I'd already thrown them to see if I should like you or not, and they said I should, so that kind of overrides the other thing, don't you reckon? I mean, if I like you, then I should help you." He grins at her. "So, ask away!"

"Wait a minute," she says. "What do you mean, the dice told you you should like me?"

"Over six, I'd like you, six and under, I wouldn't. You got eleven. So I like you."

"You can't like people just on the throw of dice!"

"Why not? Seems to me it's as good a reason as most."

Vicky is sitting up now, staring at him. "I think that's pretty weird!"

"Weird is my middle name," Brenton says. "Didn't you know? Brenton Weird Trethewan. What did you want to ask?"

She has to admit that she's finding him funny, and even though she would prefer to be liked because she is likable rather than because the dice say she should be, it's a relief to be liked at all.

"You won't ask me what I want them for?"

"Absolutely not!" he promises.

"Have you got some old clothes I can have?"

"Whatever you want. The shirt off my back if you like." He begins to take it off.

"No," she says with a giggle. "That won't be necessary. Just an old shirt and a pair of shorts, and some thongs."

"I'll go and see what I can find."

He returns in a few minutes with an old white T-shirt, a pair of denim shorts and some very shabby thongs. "These do?"

"They're great! Thanks!"

"No worries. And now, back to the Labyrinth. If I disappear look for me at the bottom of the Thousand Steps, that's what I'm trying next. Are you going to have a sleep?"

"I'm trying not to go to sleep, because then I wake up in the middle of the night."

He gives her a strange look. He knows, Victoria thinks.
96 He's heard me crying. Oh please, don't let him say anything.

He doesn't. He merely smiles at her again enigmatically, throws the dice in the air and catches them. Then he goes out of the room, closing the door quietly behind him.

58 A FEW minutes later Victoria opens the door equally quietly and tiptoes down the passage to the front door. From the back of the house she can hear the whir of the sewing machine stopping and starting, and there is a delicious smell of something baking, which after a moment she recognizes as mince pies. It reminds her of Christmas and celebration and excitement.

It's not only the thought of Christmas that makes her heart beat a little faster as she opens the front door of the house, crosses the veranda and plunges boldly out into the afternoon heat. Under her arm she holds a bundle—Brenton's old clothes wrapped in a towel. She is going to the beach to meet the alien.

She is almost certain that she should tell Chris where she is going, but she doesn't want to. She wants to do something on her own that nobody else knows anything about. She does not want baby-sitting.

The vehicle is back outside the shack, and the dog is lying watchfully on the step. Victoria hurries along the road to the township, and then doubles back along the beach.

The sea is well up, deep enough to get comfortably wet in. About halfway between the jetty and the caves, Victoria stops, takes off her clothes, revealing the swimsuit she put on earlier, makes a pile of them on the sand next to the other bundle and runs into the water.

It is shallow and miraculously clear. With her face close **97** to the surface she can see to the bottom as if through a mask. The underwater world springs into being as though it has been enchanted and was only waiting for her to observe it to become real. Tiny transluscent fish flit to and fro, the entire shoal moving as one. Crabs scuttle across the seafloor, and a dozen different varieties of seaweed have put on new and glowing colors with the return of the water and are standing up and dancing.

Lying on her stomach, supporting herself on her fingertips, Victoria glides slowly, a visitor from another dimension spying on the microcosmic world below. The sea is still winter cold, however, and she is soon shivering. Reluctantly she leaves the underwater world. Wrapping the towel around her and picking up the two sets of clothes, she walks toward the caves.

He is waiting for her. They look tentatively at each other across the vast distances of time and space that usually lie between them and now no longer do. Victoria is conscious of a huge gulf of difference she is not sure she will ever be able to bridge.

"Here are some clothes," she offers diffidently.

"Thanks!" The word has a little extra twist of meaning that they are both aware of. It is one of the first words he received from her and now he is returning it. "Thanks for the radio too. I won't need it anymore."

"What did you need it for?" she asks as they make their exchange.

He shows her the silver card. "This works as a language scanner, among other things. It's like what you call a computer. It analyzed your language from the radio and put it into my mind."

"How does it work?" she inquires curiously, but when
98 he tries to explain it to her, she understands it no more than

she would quantum mechanics—less in fact. She has simply no terms of reference to hang the explanation onto. It is like a person blind from birth trying to understand the color blue. Cal laughs kindly, squats down on his heels and pats the sand next to him, a gesture simple enough for her to grasp. She sits down next to him. Talking slowly and clearly he says, "What do you call the process by which you make things like the radio?"

"The process?" Victoria wrinkles up her nose and thinks. "Technology, I suppose."

He lifts the card, stares at it for a moment and nods. "Yes, technology. Well, we use something similar to what you call technology. It's not really anything like it, but it's the same sort of thing. We use different forms of energy."

"Sunlight," she hazards, thinking of the photosynthesizer.

"Sunlight, and sundark, and . . . other things. I can't explain it to you; as far as I can tell your language has no names for our sources of energy. They have probably never occurred to your civilization."

"Where is your civilization? Where do you come from?"

Again he tries to explain to her and again she cannot grasp the concept. Having always been considered, by herself and others, a clever person, Victoria finds it frustrating and vaguely alarming. It reminds her of when she was lost in Willstown; she was so certain she had to turn right when she came out of Rawlings', and when she realized she should have gone left, it was as though someone had turned the whole town back to front just to mislead her.

One night in Nigeria her father had shown some slides on the outside wall of the veranda. The "watchnight," Isafu, had come over to see them. He had never been away from Kano. He had no concept of Australia as a different country. **99**

He thought the snow on Mt. Kosciusko was a sort of white sand. She and Simon had thought that was really incredible; they had privately thought the old man rather stupid. . . . Now Victoria realizes that to the strange boy sitting next to her on the sand she seems just as stupid and ignorant, just as primitive and quaint. She cannot understand where he has come from: he is from some totally different dimension that has never occurred to her.

She gives up on that one, and asks, "What are you doing here?"

"I study people patterns. You would probably call me a sort of anthropologist. There is a tribe in this area that I have been interested in for some time. I wanted to make comparisons with some fieldwork done in another part of this continent. And I needed a holiday, a break from routine. So I thought I would make a back-to-nature trip." He smiles, a little self-mockingly, and she suddenly sees him, not as a boy, but as an adult, wise, experienced and educated.

"What sort of tribe?"

"They call themselves the Narrangga."

"Aborigines? There aren't any Aboriginal tribes here anymore. They've all gone."

"I know," he agrees, in the irritating manner of someone who knows everything. "I gathered that from the radio. Both the apparatus and its content presuppose an entirely different civilization. It's rather annoying. I am in the right place, geographically, but in the wrong time. The transport technicians must have miscalculated one of the variables and landed me in your time by mistake." He pauses as though deep in thought.

"What will you do?" Vicky ventures.

"What I *should* do, what the instructions always tell you to do, is return immediately. I should have done that already, as soon as I saw the first artifacts you gave me. They told me at once I was in the wrong era. But I was very excited. As far as I know, no one has ever visited this time span. We are warned off trying to reach it; it is considered on the one hand to be too boring and on the other too dangerous. And this civilization is comparatively short-lived, which makes it hard to pinpoint, unlike the Narrangga, who remained in the same place for thousands and thousands of years. Many people believe that it never actually existed, that your civilization is only a myth. I shall be able to go back and prove them all wrong." He smiles in professional satisfaction, just as Victoria's parents do, and says, "You can be my guide. You can take me to where you live."

This suggestion alarms Victoria considerably. "It's rather difficult," she begins hesitantly.

"Explain to me why," he commands. "Remember, I am interested in all aspects of your culture. Is there some kind of taboo? Are strangers ostracized? I hope they are not sacrificed. That was a joke," he adds a little nervously, allowing a dry smile to flicker across his face.

"No, nothing like that. It's just that they'll wonder where you've come from, and ask all kinds of questions, especially since you're . . ." she pauses, not wanting to offend him, and then, reasoning that he will take it scientifically, continues, "since you're black."

"Black? You mean black-eyed? You have some special superstition about black-eyed people?"

"No, not eyes. Skin."

He looks a little surprised. "But my skin is not black, it is brown."

"People call it black. And they're going to think you're an Aborigine, like the Narrangga."

"Does it make any difference?"

"It shouldn't," Vicky says sadly, "but I'm afraid it might."

Cal is looking at her skin, naturally sallow and now tanned dark by the African sun. It is only a couple of shades lighter than his. "You are not a Narrangga?" he says hopefully. She shakes her head. "And you are not 'black'?"

"No."

"What are you then?"

"I am a European, I suppose," she answers, "and I would be described as white."

He wants to get it quite clear. "Europeans do not have dark skins?"

Victoria laughs, but rather grimly. The whole conversation is making her sad, but it seems funny that he should not know about it. "Some of them are quite dark," she says, "but they are still called white. They're all sorts of colors, but they are paler than black people, and they have different faces and lighter eyes."

"How fascinating," Cal says. "I've always maintained it is so important actually to visit one's field of study. It's always the obvious, the self-evident, that escapes one otherwise. The things that no one bothers to mention because everyone knows them. This explains to me why the other person, Micky, is the color he is. I thought the poor thing was suffering from a skin disease. Occasionally our people grow without pigmentation, but they are not permitted to develop." He shakes his head in wonder and continues, "The idea is so bizarre. It's always been assumed that the only color for people is brown."

"It's definitely not that way here," Victoria tells him. "The other thing is . . ." she gives him a look. "Well, how old are you?"

He is greatly offended by this. He looks away from her
and says in an embarrassed voice, "Is it necessary to tell?"

"For heaven's sake, it doesn't really matter," she says. "But I'd better warn you everyone's going to think you're a kid, a child, someone who's not grown-up yet. Because that's what you look like."

Cal is silent for a few moments as he absorbs this information. For a moment he looks quite distant as though he has already decided to leave. But then a look that is almost mischievous comes into his eyes, and he says to Vicky, "But you are a child, aren't you? So I can come with you and be your friend? I will not be noticed too much." He has recovered from the shock of being asked his age. He gets to his feet and smiles at her. "Come on," he says.

Victoria is aware of a slight pressure on her. She stands up too, wondering how she is going to explain coming home with a friend she has met on the beach, whom everyone is going to assume is something quite different from what he really is.

"You'd better change clothes," she suggests.

He picks them up and holds them out. A wrinkle of distaste crosses his face.

"What's wrong?" Vicky asks.

"They smell very strange," he admits. "But never mind, never mind. It's quite unimportant. I will get used to it. How do they go?"

"This one goes over your head," she explains, pointing to the T-shirt. "Your arms go through the sleeves. And you step into the shorts, one leg in each hole."

He begins to struggle awkwardly with the T-shirt. Victoria says, "Hadn't you better take off your own clothes first?"

He looks a little anxious at this. "These are not only clothes," he informs her. "They also give me protection against other things, cold, heat, illness and so on."

"You'll be a lot more noticeable with them on," she says. **103**

He hesitates for a moment, and then, with the same look of daring in his eyes, says, "I can't back out now! I'd never forgive myself if I didn't go through with it. Here goes!"

He touches the material at his throat, and as it comes apart he casually steps out of it.

Underneath he is naked, his skin brown and smooth. Victoria turns away quickly, embarrassed, but not before she has seen very clearly that *he* is not a boy at all. The alien's body has not got a penis like Victoria's brother, Simon, and all the other boys. It is shaped just like Victoria's own. The alien is female!

This final shock is more than Victoria can take. Somehow it seems more extraordinary than all the rest put together. It makes her realize a flood of different things at once. She assumed Cal was a boy because of *his* manner of dealing with the world, so confident and assured. She had assumed people in any culture who were anthropologists and explorers were automatically male. She feels thrown off balance by having related to someone as a boy when all the time *he* was a girl. She sees all at once the limitations she places on herself, simply because she is female. And she feels very strongly a new resentment toward Michael, who avoids her not because he dislikes her but because she is a girl.

She suddenly understands the need to swear to relieve her feelings. She says the worst thing she allows herself. "Oh bloody hell!"

Cal, dressed now in Brenton's shorts and T-shirt, has sat down to try to fit the thongs over her toes. She looks up quickly. "What's the matter?"

"That's not the way to put them on," Vicky says. "You stand up and feel for them with your toes, like this." She **104** demonstrates, giving herself time to regain control.

"I am sorry," Cal says, standing up again. "I should have realized that taking off one's clothes would be a taboo here. I did not mean to shock you."

"You'd better not do it in front of anyone else," Vicky says, beginning to see the funny side of it. "But it's not only that. I thought you were a boy. I didn't realize you were a girl. It was rather a surprise."

"When one's race has achieved monosexuality, it is hard to understand all the complexities of bisexual races," Cal informs her.

"I'm sure it is," Vicky replies. "But you're going to have to try and understand some of them here, otherwise you'll be in trouble. Don't you have any men or boys where you come from? You're all female?"

"We only have one body shape. We do not need a word to distinguish it. We simply call ourselves . . ." She says a word that Victoria cannot grasp, and then translates it, "humans."

"But what happened to all the men?"

"I don't know exactly. It was a very long time ago."

"And babies, what about babies? How do you make new people without any men?"

Once again Victoria finds the concepts just too strange to grasp. The alien's method of reproduction sounds like a mixture between an incubator and a flowerbed. But what Victoria does get an inkling of is that Cal is not a member of half the human-race-divided-into-male-and-female, nor even half the human-race-divided-into-child-and-adult. And this gives the alien girl her remarkable air of self-sufficiency.

59 VICTORIA SHIVERS. The afternoon has stretched imperceptibly into evening and the breeze off the sea is freshening. She puts her T-shirt and shorts on over her now dry swimsuit and picks up her towel and the radio. She feels she has been concentrating harder than ever before and her brain is about to go on strike. She wants to get away completely from the alien concepts she has been trying to grapple with. She thinks she will just tell Cal firmly, "Good-bye," and go home, but as she is opening her mouth something happens to make her change her mind.

From up the beach, in the direction of the shack, comes the sound of voices. Vicky looks toward them and sees the woman from the shack and a man, her husband presumably, stepping down from the rocks onto the beach. They have plastic buckets and knives in their hands, and the man carries a spade. They must be going to look for bait. She looks at Cal, no longer protected by camouflage, a skinny black child in Brenton's old clothes, and she feels a rush of concern for her. Cal looks so confident and composed; she has no idea how vulnerable she is. She has no idea that in this culture she is just about at the bottom of the kicking order.

"Come on!" Vicky says urgently, and takes her by the hand. This time Cal does not flinch and recoil from the touch. Her hand is thin and cold in Vicky's.

"Run," Vicky orders. She thinks, as they take off, that she hears a voice shout behind them, "Hey, you kids! Come here!" but the wind whips the words away.

60

THEIR PROGRESS is not as fast as she would like. Cal has no idea how to run in thongs, and she keeps stumbling over them. In fact she does not seem to have much of an idea how to run at all. Her legs are straight when they should bend and give way when they should be rigid, and her arms swing the wrong way. The two girls quickly slow to a walk. Cal is breathing hard and her black eyes are large.

"I could use a transport wave," she says. "I wanted to get back to nature, but this walking business is a bit too primitive."

"You'll have to get used to walking," Vicky says. "There's no other way to get around."

"But you have other forms of transport?"

"Yes, cars." They are close to the seawall at the township now and Victoria points to a sedan and a pickup truck parked with their noses toward the sea. "Those are cars. But only grown-ups are allowed to drive them. Children mostly walk or ride bicycles."

"What energy source powers the cars?" Cal wants to know.

"They run on petrol, which comes from oil. It's found underground; it's a fossil fuel."

"Mineral slime!" Cal says in delight. "Now *that* I always thought was a myth. I couldn't believe anyone would waste time extracting a substance whose supplies were infinitesimal compared to other energy sources. Mineral slime!"

She looks warily at the steps leading up off the beach and holding onto the rail very carefully climbs gingerly up them. **107**

At the top she walks all around the sedan, admiring it. Then she tries the door, opens it and climbs in.

"Get out," Vicky begs in alarm. "That's not allowed."

As Cal is clambering clumsily out, a truck rumbles up the road and comes to a halt outside the store, its hazard lights flashing. Cal regards it, delighted. It is covered in silver badges and lights; it is a wonderful truck, huge and powerful.

"Amazing," she breathes.

A man jumps from the cabin and saunters into the store. Cal circles the truck, studying it from all angles. For some reason she finds it funny and she is grinning when she comes back.

"What are the signs on the front?"

"The numbers? That's the registration; every vehicle has to have one."

"Show me what they stand for," Cal commands.

Victoria holds up her fingers, as she points to each number. "Five, two, seven." Cal counts them off in her head and takes out the language scanner.

"You'd better explain your writing system to me too."

Apart from the three letters on the truck's registration plate the only other examples of writing are the advertisements on the walls and window of the store. Victoria regards them with some dismay; they do not seem to be a very accurate source of information. Nevertheless she reads them out to Cal. "Balfour's Pies and Cakes. Street's Ice Cream. Come to Marlboro Country. Coke, It's the Real Thing."

Cal sways on her feet a little, and her chrysanthemum head droops slightly. "These are all foods, things to eat?" As she approaches the window her nose wrinkles in distaste and she mutters something to herself in her own language. 108 The plastic strips in the doorway sway violently apart and the truck driver comes out. He is a large man with a good-sized beer gut hanging over his bluejeans and hardly concealed at all by a blue undershirt. Cal gives a half-suppressed cry and leaps backward, tripping over the unaccustomed thongs and falling to the ground.

The truck driver surveys her in surprise, but not unkindly. "What's the matter, Tiger? In too much of a hurry to get your candy?"

Before he gets back in the truck he takes a cigarette out, puts it between his lips and lights it. Cal watches fascinated, getting to her feet without taking her eyes off him.

"Ain't you ever seen anyone light up before?" he asks her, with a wink at Victoria. He inhales the smoke with pleasure and blows it out in a ring.

"Here." He puts his hand in his pocket and takes out a coin. He holds it out to Cal, but she merely stares at him without moving, her eyes sliding sideways to seek Vicky's help.

"Don't be shy!" He takes her hand and puts the coin in it. Her eyes are almost popping out of her head as she looks up at him. "Buy yourself an ice cream," he tells her, lets go of her hand, gives Victoria another wink and vaults into the driver's seat. The truck's engine comes to life with a roar.

Cal opens her hand and looks at the coin. Then she looks at Vicky and laughs, but while she laughs she is also shivering, and Vicky realizes she has had a real fright.

"So that was a man," Cal says. Her voice is detached and scientific, but she can't help opening her eyes wide at the same time.

"I suppose he looked huge to you?"

"Very big!" Cal agrees. "Why did he give me this?" She shows the fifty-cent coin to Vicky.

"That's a piece of money," Victoria explains. "You have to have money to buy the things in the shops."

"Ah!" This simple sentence seems to mean a lot to Cal. She lifts the language scanner again and looks intently at it for a few moments.

"What are you doing?"

"I'm building up a schema—a picture of your society. Whenever I learn something I put it in the scanner."

"But how do you actually put it in?"

"It picks up the brain impulses and records them. You might say I am telling it with my mind. It's very simple, but it seems hard to you, because there are many things that you don't seem to know. You don't seem to use your minds in that particular way. And yet, the Narrangga used to in their own way, we believe. The information must have been lost somewhere."

Her tone of voice is scientific, but there's also a note in it that is faintly patronizing. Victoria feels very inferior, and another thought occurs to her.

"Can you tell what I'm thinking?"

Cal considers her with a beady black eye, looking like a very intelligent crow. "Not really," she admits. "You would have to have the ability to transmit messages clearly. What comes from you is very muddled." She looks a little shame-faced and adds, "I apologize. I did not mean to insult you."

"You didn't insult me," Victoria answers. "I don't mind."

"With us it's very rude to accuse someone of being muddled. We call it being a 'victim of the old brain'—that's a rough translation, of course." Cal smiles, looking less like a professor and more like a kid. "I am often called it," she confides in Vicky. "I am considered very hotheaded and impulsive."

110   She has been feeling the coin throughout this conver-

sation, running her fingers around its edge and peering at the engravings on its surface. Now she asks, "What am I supposed to do with this?"

"He just said you could buy yourself an ice cream with it."

"Ice cream? To eat?" Once more the droopy look comes over Cal. "Do I have to?"

"You don't have to. You can do what you like with the money. He was just being kind. He probably thought you looked half starved," Vicky adds, looking at Cal's skinny figure.

"It's not some sort of custom, and he'll not be upset if I don't do it?" Cal persists.

"He won't even know. You'll probably never see him again."

"He wasn't one of your men? One of your tribe?"

Vicky shakes her head and sighs. "I don't think I can explain everything to you all at once," she says wearily. Suddenly she feels tired and hungry, and she wonders if anyone at the Trethewans' is missing her. "We'd better go back to my place," she continues uncertainly. She doesn't think Cal is capable of looking after herself on her own, despite being from such a highly advanced culture. "Don't ask too many questions, and if there's anything you don't understand, pretend to be shy, and I'll answer for you."

"I'm not sure I know what shy means," Cal replies. "But I suppose I can try to be it."

61 "HOW beautiful it looks!"

By the time the two girls get to the house Cal is exhausted and limping, but this doesn't stop her enthusing over the old pines around the homestead, the rather scrappy gum trees in the paddocks and the green lawns and flowers that surround the house. At the sight of the animals she grips Vicky's arm in excitement. "What are those things?"

"The ones with four legs are called goats," Vicky explains carefully, trying not to giggle. "And the two-legged ones are chickens, also known as chooks. Don't you have any animals?" she goes on curiously.

"Very few," Cal replies, gazing raptly at the Anglo-Nubians. "There used to be more, long ago, but most of them became extinct. Where I come from there is no longer any natural habitat for other life-forms. It is all controlled for human living."

Vicky puts her hand over the fence and lets one of the nanny goats lick her fingers. "You can stroke them if you like," she says. "They won't hurt you."

But Cal is reluctant to touch them. She explains with a half-embarrassed smile, "Everything smells so terrible. I'm surprised you can stand it."

"You'll get used to it," Vicky says. "But don't mention it to anyone else."

The goats are hungry. They bleat plaintively as the girls cross the yard to the kitchen door. As the screen door slams, 112 the chickens start up their predinner clucking too. The evening sun has been slanting into Vicky's eyes, and inside the kitchen she can hardly see. Once she gets her vision back she notices that Cal has again started to wilt.

"What's wrong?" she whispers urgently.

"Terrible smell," Cal mouths back.

It is of mince pies, mouth-watering and delicious, heralding Christmas. Vicky is sniffing it appreciatively when Chris comes into the kitchen from the sewing room.

"Vicky, I was beginning to wonder where you were." She looks at Cal, tries to hide her surprise and doesn't quite manage it. "Hello!" she says, rather suspiciously.

"Hello," Cal replies carefully, and gives a slow, cautious smile, showing her tiny white teeth.

Victoria has a feeling she is diving into deep dark water with a strong possibility she will break her neck on the bottom and drown. She plunges in nonetheless.

"This is Cal. I met her on the beach." She stops, not knowing how to continue without straying too far from the truth.

"Hi, Cal." For the time being Chris's natural politeness is going to override her suspicions. She smiles at the dark-skinned girl and, for the sake of saying something, asks, "Are you here on holiday?"

"Yes," Cal replies in a serious voice. She is as fascinated by Chris as by the goats. She cannot take her eyes off her.

The scrutiny makes Chris a little uncomfortable. She sounds slightly more hostile now as she says, "Where do you come from?"

Cal gives a remarkable attempt at a shy giggle, and looks sideways at Vicky, who replies quickly for her. "She's from the city."

"Oh, which part?" Chris goes on. "I grew up in the city."

113

Vicky's mind has gone quite blank. For a moment she can't even remember the name of the suburb she used to live in. Luckily after a moment's invisible consultation with the langscan Cal replies rather triumphantly, "Collins-wood!"

"Oh, near the ABC," Chris remarks. "I don't know that part very well. Would you like a mince pie?" She indicates the cake rack on the table, where several dozen mince pies are cooling.

"No. I shouldn't try them, they might be poisonous for me," Cal says politely.

Chris looks at her sharply to see if she is being funny. "I don't think they're that bad!" she says, sounding a little offended. Victoria puts in hastily, "I'd love one." Then she adds, "Cal can't eat mince pies, she's . . . she's allergic to sugar!"

"Oh you poor thing," Chris exclaims. "Is that why you're so thin? Are you allergic to anything else?"

"Everything," Cal says solemnly. Once again Chris is not sure if she's joking or not. "But I need to drink," Cal continues. "Would you give me something to drink, please?"

Chris is the sort of mother who loves to offer children food and drink but doesn't like it when they demand things. Her voice is getting frostier as she tells Vicky to get some apple juice for them both out of the fridge.

Cal sniffs at the juice and sips it warily. She doesn't seem to be too keen on it, but at least she doesn't spit it out, nor does she pass any more comments. Victoria drinks her apple juice more quickly, enjoying the cold, sweet liquid, and then she eats two mince pies.

Just as she is swallowing the last one, Brenton bursts into

the kitchen. "Mince pies! The whole house is smelling of

mince pies. It's brought on acute mince-pie deprivation syndrome. Quick, give me one before I die!"

"Just one, Brenton," Chris orders. "They're for tonight when we decorate the Christmas tree."

"What's that?" Cal whispers to Victoria.

"I'll tell you later," she whispers back.

"How many did Vicky have?" Brenton demands.

"Two," she confesses.

"Then I can have two, too! Equal rights, Mum! Vicky is not a visitor, she is one of the family. If she has two, I have two!"

He takes one in each hand, exclaims a little because they are hot and crams them into his mouth. Cal has transferred her gaze from Chris to Brenton, and their eyes now meet for the first time.

"Ouf!" Brenton gasps. There is a moment of sudden intensity during which some swift interchange takes place between Cal and Brenton. He is so astonished by it that he immediately begins to choke on the mince pies.

"Serves you right!" His mother regards him unsympathetically. "Fancy trying to eat two at once like that. You'd better have a drink. Vicky, pour one out for him."

Vicky looks from Brenton, who has tears in his eyes from spluttering, to Cal. The alien girl is staring at him with intense and startled interest.

"Thanks." Brenton drinks the apple juice and, recovering, says casually but not very naturally to Cal, "Where did you spring from?"

"She and Vicky met on the beach," Chris says. She is washing up the mince-pie trays and putting them back in the oven to dry. "I must do something about dinner," she remarks to no one in particular, looking distractedly at the kitchen clock. "I had no idea it was so late. Geoff **115** will be back in a minute. Brenton, can you please do the animals?"

"We'll all do them!" He surprises her by jumping to his feet immediately. "Come on, Vicky, bring Cal outside. We'll show her around."

"I would like to see the inside too," Cal says, smiling delightedly and managing to look more like a professor than ever.

"OK," Brenton says, giving her no more than a flicker of a glance. "We'll show you the house and then we'll do the animals."

As soon as they are out of the kitchen he hisses to Victoria, "Why is she wearing my clothes?"

"She . . . she needed something to wear after swimming," Victoria improvises weakly. Brenton fixes her with a justly contemptuous stare. "You always were a hopeless liar, Vicky Hare!"

"You said you wouldn't ask," she reminds him.

"The question I said I wouldn't ask was an entirely different one."

"I can't tell you," Victoria returns stubbornly.

He frowns and looks behind her to where Cal has advanced as far as the family room and is examining the television with interest. She turns and calls to Vicky, "What is this?"

"Haven't you seen a TV before?" Brenton asks, looking as though he is trying to work out a very complicated puzzle in his head.

"Ah, TV. Switch it on!"

"Bossy girl," Brenton observes, but he crosses to the television and switches it on. The last moments of a Road Runner cartoon are followed by a commercial for barbecued potato chips. Cal squints at these cultural offerings in some

116 bewilderment.

"You can't see it properly, can you?" Brenton says acutely.

"Two-dimensional images are hard for me," she admits, "especially moving ones. Our images are multidimensional."

"Whatever that means," Brenton retorts sarcastically, and gives her a long, suspicious look. She returns the look calmly, ignoring Victoria, who is making anxious gestures at her behind Brenton's back. Again there is the same moment of intense concentration between the boy and the dark-skinned girl, and again it is Brenton who looks away uneasily.

"You want to see my room?" he suggests.

He enters the room first and crosses to his bed, sits down on it and draws his knees up under his chin. Victoria leans against the doorjamb. Cal glances around the room and notices the nuclear weapons collection. She looks puzzled and walks across the room to peer at the posters more closely.

"What are these?"

"Nuclear weapons," Brenton replies. A short silence follows during which the puzzlement on Cal's face slowly turns to revulsion. Then Brenton asks, "Do you know what they are?"

She nods slowly. "I have heard of them." Her face as she looks from Brenton to Victoria is full of sorrowful pity, and they find this look far more frightening than all the pictures of weapons put together. The luminous evening air darkens and the warmth of the sun diminishes. Cal loses her remote alien look and for a moment becomes simply a human being like the others, sharing their fear.

"What do you know about them?" Brenton asks with an urgency he does not altogether understand.

"Not much," she replies, glancing at the posters again. "Not as much as you." With an almost conscious effort she   *117* reverts once again to being the observer. Her scientific air returns and she makes a point of not looking at either of them.

She looks instead around the room. The next thing that catches her attention is one of the Burmese cats, curled up on Brenton's pillow. She approaches it warily and stares at it, making no attempt to touch it.

"It's a cat," Victoria explains helpfully.

"Of course it's a cat!" Brenton remarks scornfully. "Everyone knows what cats are!"

The cat opens its pink mouth and yowls questioningly, wondering who the stranger is. Brenton picks it up. "Come and say hello to Cal!" He holds the cat swiftly out toward her. Cal draws back involuntarily, in a mixture of fascination and disgust. The disgust is apparently shared by the cat. It gives a banshee wail and spits furiously, leaps out of Brenton's arms and makes a dash for the door.

"He doesn't like you," Brenton says, sucking the back of his hand where Tang's claws scratched the skin. "Isn't that strange?"

"I must have frightened him. I hope I didn't upset him too badly," Cal says, looking at the posters on the wall. A rather uneasy silence follows while each person in the room wonders what to say next. Victoria is wondering if she should tell Brenton who Cal really is. She can see that he has already begun to suspect something, and she knows that, single-minded as he is, he will not give up until he has discovered the truth.

Wanting to postpone that moment, she picks up the *Labyrinth of Dead Ends* from the bed and says to him, "How's the game going?"

"It's getting very dodgy," he replies. "I've run out of luck completely, and I think I'm about to be betrayed by a so-called ally."

"What game is it?" Cal asks with interest. Brenton shows her the dice and the pieces of paper he has been making notes on. "It's a sort of role-playing fantasy game. You read the book and play that you're actually in the story. I'll show you where I've got to this time." He takes the book from Victoria, flicks through the pages and hands it back to Cal. She squints her black eyes at it and shoots a *help me* glance at Victoria.

"I'll read it to you." Vicky leans over her shoulder.

"You have reached the top of the thousand steps, but the climb has left you seriously weakened. You must either eat some of your provisions or share your companions' victuals. The Viking offers you a drink from his cow-horn flask. The Amazon offers you a handful of dried fruits. If you eat the dried fruits turn to page 173. If you drink from the flask turn to page 46. If you eat your own provisions subtract two from your score and turn to page 210. . . .

"What are you going to do, Brenton?"

"I think I'll take the drink from the Viking. My score's getting really low. Vikings are usually honorable types."

Vicky turns the page, showing Cal what she is doing. "Bad luck!" She reads some more:

"The Viking smiles in satisfaction knowing that he has laced the drink with foxglove poison. You will be dead within an hour."

Brenton swears mildly, but at the moment he's much more interested in Cal. "Can't she read?" he says disbelievingly to Victoria. "Don't you think she's a pretty weird person?" He has taken the dice out of his pocket and is tossing them up and down in his palm. But before he can **119** say anything further, Chris shouts to them from the kitchen. "Can you kids get a move on and feed those animals?"

62 BRENTON fetches hay and pellets for the goats, and Victoria mixes up mash for the chickens. Cal ambles around the yard watching them and admiring the garden and the flowers. The goats give her a wide berth and roll their slanted yellow eyes in alarm if she approaches them. Brenton is observing this in silence when they hear the noise of a car approaching, and the Commodore comes tearing up the drive, skidding to a halt outside the shed. Michael jumps from the front seat, hair wet, face sunburned. He catches sight of Cal, does an exaggerated double take and saunters across.

"Did you bring back my radio?" He speaks very slowly and clearly as though to a half-wit.

"I brought it back," Vicky tells him. "It's on the kitchen table."

"Hello, Micky," Cal says carefully, and then to Geoff, who has come across to join them, "Are you their father?"

There is something wrong with the way she says it. Everyone notices it. It sounds too adult, too confident, too superior. Geoff raises his eyebrows mildly but doesn't say anything. He looks past Cal at the goats in the paddock. "That nanny's enormous," he comments. "She must be about to pod."

They all look at the distended flanks and swollen teats of the nanny goat. Cal gives a shudder and looks again at 120 Geoff. Next to him she looks small and insubstantial, but she is not daunted by his size. She inquires again, "You are obviously Michael's father. There is a likeness. But what about these two?"

"Both the boys are mine." Geoff is about to make a joke of it, but he can't resist adding a sting too. "Though I sometimes wonder about Brenton. We just borrowed the girl for a bit."

"Borrowed?" Cal frowns. She says to Vicky, "Is that a local custom?"

"He means I'm just staying with them," Vicky explains. "My parents live a long way away and I have to go to school here."

It doesn't seem to her like a very good explanation, but it satisfies Cal for the time being; she returns to the vexing question of the two dissimilar brothers. "They had the same mother?" she asks their father.

"Bloody hell!" Geoff swears impatiently. "Ease off a bit, will you, kid? Not so many questions."

"I am sorry," she answers. "I apologize." But it's not said the way a kid would say it; it's said like an adult, equal to equal. Geoff gives her a hard look to see if she's being cheeky, but before he can decide if she is or not, there's the noise of another car approaching, and the 4WD from the shack pulls up.

"How are you, Geoff?" Pam calls to him from the driver's seat.

"Going good, thanks, Pam. How about you?"

"Not too bad. Getting there, I suppose. I just came up to tell you we'll be putting the net out for the next few evenings. You kids, stay away from it if you're swimming down there. You never know with sharks coming after the fish . . ."

"Right," Geoff agrees a little too heartily. "You hear that, **121** kids? No swimming near the net. Thanks for letting us know."

"Well, to tell you the truth," Pam continues, looking hard at Cal, "I saw the little girl leaving the beach with the black kid, and I just wanted to check if she got home all right. I wouldn't let her wander around on her own so much if I was you. You can't be too careful these days."

"Aw, she's all right," Geoff says easily, but Pam is not going to be brushed off lightly. "I didn't know there were any Aboriginal families around here," she persists. "Where are you from, boy?"

"She's not a boy, she's a girl," Brenton intervenes, and then notices Michael's look of utter astonishment. It fazes him for a moment, but he quickly recovers and goes on. "She's here on holiday and she's staying at the caravan park. And she's not an Aborigine anyway." Having none of Victoria's strict regard for truth, he lies quite convincingly.

Pam narrows her eyes as she stares at him. "She's adopted, is she? I'm just going down to the caravan park. Hop in, kid. I'll give you a ride."

Geoff is starting to say "That's good of you," but Brenton interrupts. "She's not going yet." He winks at Victoria. "Come on!" he says shortly at her and Cal, picks up the buckets and hustles them across the yard to the shed. Michael looks after them, his face puzzled. Geoff gives Pam a final wave and, as the 4WD roars away down the drive, he puts his arm across his younger son's shoulders. "Come on, mate. Let's go and get ourselves a drink!"

63 IN THE shed Brenton slings the buckets into the corner and turns to face Victoria. "Come on," he commands. "Out with it! Where does she really come from?" Then he swings abruptly toward Cal and hisses, "Who are you?"

Victoria says with mixed feelings, "I don't know. I can't really understand. But she's not from here. She's from . . . somewhere else." Then she finishes rather helplessly, because it sounds so idiotic, "She's an alien."

Brenton starts to laugh but as he turns toward Cal something stops him in his tracks. He stops laughing abruptly and gasps, the way he did in the kitchen. Cal is regarding him with benevolent interest as though he is a pet dog who has just performed a particularly clever trick.

"Very good," she says complacently.

"How do you do that?" Brenton asks, shaking his head as though he has just woken up.

"How does she do what?" Vicky interrupts, a little put out that the two of them are ignoring her completely.

"She plugs into your mind," Brenton explains. "She knows what you're thinking, and she tells you what she's thinking."

"She doesn't do it to me," Vicky complains.

"You are transmitting very clearly," Cal tells Brenton approvingly. "I am surprised; it is most interesting. And now, I must get back to my things. I need my own clothes. Something has been biting me and I may prove allergic to it." She rubs the back of her neck.

"Mosquitoes," Vicky says. She can hear them whining around her too. "I'll take you back to the beach."

"Not yet," Brenton says excitedly. "I want to talk to her some more. What's she here for? Has she come to help us in some way?"

"I don't think so," Vicky replies. "She's not some sort of savior. She's just an anthropologist, and she came here by mistake. She came to study the Narrangga, but they aren't here anymore. We're here instead."

"An anthropologist?" Brenton repeats, disappointed. "Is that all?" He turns to Cal and demands, "But what did you come to study the Narrangga for? And where do you come from?"

"See if you can grasp it," Cal says, looking at him directly. There is a brief, silent exchange, then Brenton drops his gaze, clutches at his head with both hands and moans.

"Whatever's the matter?" Vicky demands.

"It's all right," he says, looking at her and laughing rather helplessly. "It's just my mind being expanded. It hurts!"

"But what's she saying?"

Brenton opens his mouth to speak but no words come, and after a few seconds he closes it again, looking confused. "I thought I understood it perfectly, but when I try to put it into words it all gets muddled. Something to do with collecting patterns of behavior . . . rhythm . . . the spaces between things . . . between people . . ." His voice trails away and he glances at Cal. "But that's not really anything like it, is it?"

"I would have to live among you for a long time to explain it properly to you in your own terminology," she replies. "I would need to know your language and culture intimately and deeply. At the moment I only know it on the surface.

It is true, I am a collector, and my special area is in the

patterns that form between people in their relationships. All of these things have colors to us, many different shades that combine very beautifully. We travel through all the dimensions, searching for new and exotic color patterns."

Brenton is frowning at this unlikely concept. "But what do you use them *for*?"

Cal smiles a little sadly. "Your question, and the way you use that word *for*, indicate a great deal about your society to me."

"I guess we don't make very nice patterns," he says, a little ashamed.

"The patterns are faint and colorless. The spaces between you are huge and empty, as though each of you is quite separate from anyone else. It is most unusual."

"And most unpleasant?"

"As an anthropologist I cannot say if it is pleasant or unpleasant, only that it is interesting."

"Interesting enough to stay here?" Brenton says eagerly.

"I will stay as long as possible, even though it is so primitive here," Cal replies. "The opportunity is too good to waste." She doesn't sound as enthusiastic as she did, and Vicky looks at her in concern.

"Are you homesick?" When Cal nods her head slightly and says, "That is not quite the word for it, but, yes, perhaps a little," Vicky says with a rush, "I am too!"

"Better to be homesick away from home than at home," Brenton says bitterly.

The three of them stand in silence for a moment, until the increasing attacks of mosquitoes remind Vicky that Cal needs to get back to her things.

"Do you think you can walk back to the beach?" she asks her, looking doubtfully at her feet. The thongs have rubbed between her toes and one foot is bleeding.

125

"Perhaps she can ride a bike?" Brenton suggests. "We'll cycle her down."

But Cal cannot ride a bike. She cannot even keep her balance when Brenton steadies the bike. After the first wobbling effort she will not take her feet off the ground. When Brenton and Victoria demonstrate the art of bike riding, she watches them in amazement, as though they are monkeys in a circus.

Their performance is interrupted by Michael, who has been sent out by his mother to announce that it's time to eat. "And you're to tell that girl to go home," he adds rather sourly. "Mum says!"

"Oh, but we have to go with her," Brenton shouts. "We'll only be a few minutes!"

64 THE TROUBLE starts when Brenton and Victoria are late for dinner. By the time they have escorted the hobbling Cal down to the beach, kept out of the way of the people from the shack and run back again, the meal is half over. Shelley has not appeared for dinner at all, and Chris is grumpy about both their lateness and her daughter's absence.

"I wonder why I bother preparing these lovely meals when half the time you don't notice what you're eating, and the other half you aren't even here," she grumbles, taking the meal out of the oven. Since it is a cheese soufflé it has collapsed completely. "You'll just have to eat flat soufflé; it serves you right."

"Give us frozen pizza and pies," Michael says cheerfully.

"Mum likes to think she's feeding us properly," Brenton

explains. "It's part of her self-image as superwoman, isn't it, Mum?"

He doesn't care what he's eating. He is high on excitement, like when he has suddenly made the right move in a game and realizes nothing can stop him winning. The arrival of the alien and the thrilling exchange of thought with her have altered his view on life completely. He thought he was trapped in a dead end, but suddenly a way out has opened up in front of him, one he never dreamed possible. He gives his mother a reckless grin and laughs maniacally.

"What's the matter with you?" She is as suspicious of his good moods as of his bad ones, as well as being annoyed by his last remark.

"Nothing at all," he assures her, and winks at Victoria. The wink does not escape his parents. His father glares at him over a forkful of food, while his mother says swiftly, "Brenton, I hope you're not up to anything stupid."

"Of course I'm not," he replies, injured. "You always think the worst of me."

"I don't trust you when you get into one of your silly moods. Now calm down."

But he can't. Excitement has got him in its grip and it's going to take him higher and higher. He knows it's putting his parents on edge, but he can't stop.

Shelley and Jason turn up just before the end of the meal. They are both alight too, with a different sort of excitement that unnerves the parents even more.

"I thought you were going to help me make the mince pies," Chris reproaches her daughter.

Shelley blushes. "I was going to, but it was just so lovely over at Barbridge, we couldn't tear ourselves away, could we, Jase?"

Their eyes meet and something new comes into the at- **127** mosphere, something secret and warm between the two of them that no one else is allowed to share. It makes Chris frown and look at her daughter searchingly. Shelley shifts uncomfortably under her mother's gaze and to change the subject cries, "Let's get the dishes done quickly and decorate the tree."

Brenton and Michael disappear with the swiftness that only years of practice can give, but Jason will do anything for Shelley at the moment, even washing up, so he puts on Chris's apron and washes, Victoria dries and Shelley puts away. Chris is making coffee and heating up mince pies. This pleasing domestic harmony is shattered suddenly by the sounds of thudding and scuffling and muffled cries from the boys' room.

Jason taps the side of a glass he is washing with a spoon. "Ding ding! End of round one, fellas!"

But Chris, with an exclamation of annoyance, puts down the coffeepot and hurries up the passageway. Geoff is already there.

"What the hell is going on?"

Michael is sitting on top of Brenton, banging his head methodically on the polished floor and dripping blood all over him from his nose. Their father pulls him effortlessly off. "Get up, Brenton," he orders. "Mick, go and get yourself a handkerchief and don't drip blood on the floor." He then takes his older son by the collar and pulls his face close to his own. "If you want to fight with your brother," he says coldly and clearly, "we'll set up a fight for you outside, and the two of you can knock each other silly. But you are not going to fight in the house, do you hear?"

He lets him go with a little more force than is strictly necessary. Brenton shouts with the injustice of it, "Don't

128 blame me! What about Mick?"

"You started it," Mick says from the doorway, sniffing into a bloodstained handkerchief.

"Whatever were you fighting about anyway?" Chris demands from behind him.

They both start explaining at once. "He just suddenly jumped on me!" "He's messed up all my things. He's impossible!"

"Come on," she says placatingly. "Simmer down, both of you. Let's all have some mince pies and do the tree."

"Stuff the tree!" Brenton cries in rage.

He can't understand what happened to the excitement that buoyed him up before. It's still there, but it has turned into something more complex and more disturbing. And it's all his family's fault—Michael's for starting the fight and everyone else's for taking his side. He refuses to talk to them anymore. He will not even look at them. He throws himself down on the bed, face into the pillow.

"Just leave him alone," his father says in a voice tinged with disgust. "If he wants to sulk he can stay in his room for the evening. Are you all right, old son?" he asks Michael.

Michael nods and touches his eye experimentally. "I'm going to get a black eye," he complains.

As they return to the kitchen, Shelley and Jason jump apart. "What happened to you?" his sister asks Michael, diverting attention from herself. "I thought you were stronger than Brenton now."

"I am," Michael replies heatedly. "He just got in a lucky shot. I wasn't expecting it."

"You probably asked for it," she replies lightly. "But we can't decorate the tree without Brenton, Mum. Can I tell him he can come out now?"

"Tell him he can come out if he apologizes."

But he does not want to apologize, and he does not want to come out.

65 THE CHRISTMAS tree looks beautiful. Chris has made decorations of bread dough and glazed them golden brown. There are plaited hearts and angels of pale straw, carved wooden figures from Europe and scarlet apples on golden strings. But there are none of the things that the children have made over the years, as there used to be.

"What did you do with them?" Michael asks.

"I threw them all out," Chris says. "They had all got so old and tatty. I just wanted things that look nice."

She does not want the children to decorate the tree any-old-how, as in former years. She carefully orchestrates the proceedings so that the end result is something pleasing to her. When she brings in the mince pies it is as though she is presenting the whole scene on the tray along with them —her beautiful home, successful husband, attractive children, wonderful Christmas tree *and* delicious mince pies! As the sole representative of the audience Victoria feels she should be applauding.

Except that it's not really true, she thinks with uncomfortable clarity. The house is mortgaged. They're always worried about money. Geoff might lose his job—Victoria has heard all these problems since she has been in the house—and Brenton won't be part of her production. That makes her wonder if it's all working out all right or not. That's why she goes after him, Victoria thinks. She can't forgive him.

As it grows darker they switch on the tree lights and watch them blink faithfully on and off in the twilight. Then Geoff sets up the projector and they look at slides of the Trethewan family when the children were little. There's one of Brenton, aged about six, in a red T-shirt and blue shorts, in midjump on the beach, laughing and happy.

"Gee," Shelley comments wistfully. "What a cute little tacker Brenton used to be!"

Chris puts down her coffee cup. "I wish he'd come in. I'll go and have a word with him."

Through the hum of the projector they can hear her voice getting louder and angrier from the passageway. Then she comes back into the room and walks straight through it to the kitchen.

"He is a moron!" Shelley exclaims. "He's just spoiling everything." But, really, this night nothing can upset her. Jason is sitting on the floor by her feet. She strokes his hair. He reaches up, takes her hand and starts to caress it. She leans down and whispers in his ear; they both smile secretively.

"Shelley!" Chris speaks sharply from the door. "You'll have to send Jason home if you want me to finish this dress of yours. I must try it on you tonight."

"Ahhh!" Shelley groans. "What a terrible choice! Jason or a new dress!" She gets to her feet and, still holding his hand, pulls him up. "Come on, Jase. I'm sending you home so I can have my new dress by Christmas. But I'll come out and say good night to you."

"That'll take a couple of hours," Michael observes from where he is sitting on the floor. Shelley gives him a kick. "That's enough from you! Or I'll black your other eye!"

"Please, Shelley," her mother interrupts. "I don't want to stay up all night."

Victoria catches the note of tiredness in her voice. It **131** makes her feel she should be doing something helpful, so she gathers up the cups and plates from around the room, takes them into the kitchen and washes them up. Then there doesn't seem to be anything else to do. The evening has gone flat. Chris and Shelley are in the sewing room. Michael and his father are doing something with fishing gear in the shed. Vicky stands in the family room for a few moments watching the Christmas tree lights flash off and on. They look as though they might be full of meaning, like one of Cal's colored patterns, but she can't decipher what it is, so she decides she may as well go to bed.

 AS SHE walks past Brenton's room she hears him call out quietly, "Vicky!"

She puts her head in. "What do you want?"

He is lying on his bed, the Burmese cat curled up on his chest, the *Labyrinth of Dead Ends* facedown on the quilt next to him. "I'm starving. Do you think you could get me something to eat?"

"Do you think I should?"

"Of course I think you should or I wouldn't ask you!"

"I think your mum would really like it if you came out."

"Don't," he groans. "Don't you start too! I'm not coming out now, but go on, Vicky, get me something to eat, please."

As she returns to the kitchen she meets Shelley coming from the sewing room. Chris is calling after her daughter, "I'll be sitting up for a while, Shelley. Could you see if the children want anything, and then send them to bed?"

"OK," she calls back; then, seeing Vicky, she says, "Hi! Do you want anything else to eat?"

"Brenton wants me to get something for him," Vicky whispers. "Do you think that's all right?"

Shelley winks at her and shuts the sewing room door. "Poor little Brenton," she whispers conspiratorially. "Let's make him a feast!"

She is sparkling with happiness. Trying not to giggle she goes swiftly to the fridge and the pantry, filling a tray for her self-exiled brother.

"Open the door for me, Vicky. We'll give him a surprise."

Shelley's happiness is infectious. Victoria can feel herself catching it. By the time they get to Brenton's room they are both giggling.

"Made it!" Shelley gasps in mock relief, putting the tray down on Brenton's bed. "Move over, you great lump. There's no room for your rations."

Brenton sits up in surprise, moving Tang off his chest onto his pillow, and grinning with pleasure at the tray filled with food. There is a plate of mince pies, a leg of chicken, two homemade rolls, a jar of mayonnaise, a bag of corn chips, four fresh apricots and six dried ones. Victoria is carrying a large bottle of lemonade and some glasses.

"Shelley, you're a genius. What a fantastic meal!"

"Eat it up quickly and hide the evidence or I'll get into trouble with Dad. Do you want anything, Vick?"

Victoria discovers she is hungry again, so she helps Brenton out with the mince pies and the corn chips. Shelley puts a tape in the cassette player. The food and the music make them all start to relax. Victoria finds a rock music magazine that looks interesting and curls up on the floor to read it. Brenton shares the chicken with Tang, and the cat licks his fingers. Shelley breaks the silence by saying, "Well, come on, tell us what the fight was about."

"Don't worry about it," Brenton says. "I can't even remember myself."

133

"You gave someone a black eye for something you can't remember?"

"I didn't mean to hurt him. It just got out of hand."

Brenton does not feel any particular animosity toward his brother. He can even look at him objectively and think what a nice person Michael is. But there is something going on between them that he cannot put into thoughts, let alone words, something that can only be worked out physically, it at all. Brenton feels as though he always has to defend his position, constantly maintain his ground. Mick is always there, on his heels, threatening to overtake him, and there is never any letup, never will be, until one or the other of them leaves home.

"It's sharing a room with him," he says finally. "It means I can never get away from him. And he makes such a mess."

"Yeah," Shelley sympathizes, gazing at Michael's side of the room. "He's a pain like that. Tell Mum to say something to him."

"Not much use in that," Brenton replies, a bitter note creeping into his voice. "She always stands up for him. It's me she always goes after. You know she does, Shell. You can't deny it."

"You just get on each other's nerves. It's part of being fourteen. And part of her being forty. It's a dangerous age, according to the women's magazines!"

"She's a dangerous person," Brenton mutters. "She should be behind bars."

"She's OK, really," Shelley tells him blithely. "You just have to know how to handle her. But she does make a lot of demands on you, I'll give you that. She wants to lean on you because she can't lean on Dad, and you never give her the least little bit of support."

134   "Did you get that out of the women's magazines too?"

he inquires skeptically, but Shelley is warming to her topic. "It's true. I've been thinking about it lately. You know what he's like; he never sits down and has a conversation with her. He's always either working, or out on the boat, or drinking with his friends. She gets no companionship from him, so she looks to the next closest person—you!"

"What about you?"

She shakes her head at him. "I mean male person, dummy!"

"How come you know so much about it?"

"I use my brains. Which you might try yourself, instead of meeting everything head-on. For such a smart person, Brenton, you're sometimes incredibly thick."

"Am I smart?" he asks, deciding to let the insult pass.

"Well, of course you are!"

"I managed to get 'unsatisfactory' on most of my subjects last year," he says gloomily.

"Probably because you spent the whole year playing D & D! Anyway, the area school isn't exactly the greatest, is it? Look at Jason. Terrible grades in his end-of-the-year exams. He's never going to get into college. Heaven knows how I'll do next year. I'm terrified. And then what? Dad's dying for us all to get out and find a job, but what is there to do around here? Nothing!"

It's something Brenton tries not to think about too much. The choices seem to be between a future that's uncertain and difficult, and no future at all.

"I wish I didn't have to grow up." He amends this slightly to, "I wish there was someone I wanted to be like. I don't want to end up like Dad. I don't know what I do want to be like, but I don't want to be like him, or like Craig's father, or like Jason, or like anyone we know around here."

"What's wrong with Jason?" Shelley asks promptly.

"There's nothing wrong with him. I just don't want to be like him and work in a supermarket." He looks suspiciously at his sister. "I suppose you're in love with him?"

"Yeah, I think I might be." Shelley pauses and grins, and then continues, "Isn't it a drag?"

"Why a drag?" Brenton asks in surprise.

"I don't want to be in love with anyone yet. It's too soon. And I'm terrified—I want to be with him, and love him, and all that, but I don't want to get tied down to one person—and at the same time I keep thinking, I must make it work out with Jason, because who else is there?"

Brenton can understand what she means. Jason, good-looking, pleasant, hardworking, a great surfer and tennis player, is definitely the most eligible young man in the area—practically the only one!

"You'd better be careful then. Don't get yourself pregnant."

"Mind your own business, little brother," she returns, coloring. Brenton studies her face, realizing instantly that she and Jason are lovers. Suddenly Shelley seems like a grown-up. On the whole life has been easier for Brenton since she has been going out with Jason. It has given him a little more space in the family and her happiness has improved their relationship. But it has also distanced her from him. She is no longer one of the children, and he still is. The gulf between them has widened. She has made the step, relatively easily, into adulthood and sexuality. He still has to make it, and it seems to him to be fraught with hazards.

"What about you?" Shelley demands. "When are you going to get yourself a girlfriend?"

"All the girls I know are taller than me. I'm not exactly a hunk, you know!"

"You're kind of cute, though," Shelley teases him. "Don't you think Brenton's cute, Vicky?"

"Shut up!" he bursts out angrily, surprising himself with the intensity of his own reaction. The few minutes of closeness come to a sudden end. "Rack off!" he says. "You just talk a lot of bullshit!"

"You might at least say thanks for the food!" Shelley is unperturbed by his sudden change of mood. On the contrary she seems rather satisfied with his reaction. She grins at Vicky. "Come on, we'll leave him in peace now. You'd better go to bed, Vicky. I'll put this away and see how Mum's getting on with my dress. See you in the morning!" She gives Brenton an exaggerated wink as she closes the door.

67

IT MUST be hours later when Brenton wakes with a start. Somewhere in the room an alarm is making an insistent *beepbeepbeep*. Identifying the noise, he climbs out of bed with a groan.

The alarm is under Michael's pillow, but Michael himself is sleeping through it peacefully. Brenton shakes him hard as he fumbles under the pillow for the watch.

"What's up? What's up?" Michael mumbles sleepily.

"You moron, you left the alarm on. It woke me up." Brenton locates it and switches it off. Then he stumbles back to bed and pulls the quilt over his head. There is silence for a few moments until Michael gets noisily out of bed and puts the light on.

"Put it off! It's the middle of the night!"

"Yeah, I know—actually it's not the middle of the night, **137** it's half past three in the morning—that's when I set the alarm for—and I'm going out in the boat with Craig and his old man. I can't find my windcheater."

He looks for his jacket all over the room. By the time he has found it, got dressed and left, Brenton is wide awake. He hears the outside door close and Michael's feet crunch on the gravel as he walks down the drive. Then he can't get back to sleep. It's not only because he's thirsty and needs to pee, he's also in the grip of the same feverish excitement that got him into trouble earlier. He is thinking about Cal, about the astonishing moment when their minds clicked together and he felt at last that he had been recognized. For someone who has always been misunderstood and disliked, the feeling is irresistible, more imperative than food and drink to the starving. But at the same time he is terrified by its strength and unfamiliarity, which threaten to lead him to some unknown destination.

Finally he gets up, goes to the toilet and then to the kitchen to help himself to a drink. Opening the fridge brings Tang out from the sewing room, where he has been sleeping on top of Shelley's new dress. Brenton pours a little milk in a saucer for the cat, watches him drink it neatly and then picks him up to take him back to bed.

The cat is purring in his ear, but that does not prevent him from hearing another sound as he passes the room that used to be Michael's. It is one that he has heard before in the night, the deep muffled breathing of someone crying.

He pauses, irresolute, not sure whether to go in and comfort Victoria or pretend he has not heard her. He is curiously glad that someone else in the house is not happy. It makes him feel less lonely. Then the thought occurs to him that since they are both awake they may as well take advantage of it. He opens the door gently and whispers into the darkness, "Hey, Vicky!"

"What is it?" Her voice is husky but otherwise normal. She doesn't want him to feel sorry for her, and he doesn't. Instead he says, louder than he means to, for the excitement is getting out of control again, "Get up! Let's go and see Cal!"

68 MICHAEL walks through the silent township to the seawall. Above his head the Milky Way is splashed dazzlingly across the sky, but he does not look up at it, nor wonder about the dizzying vastness of space. He puts his hands into his pockets to keep them warm, and his fingers encounter something strange and cold. He pulls it out—it is the piece of junk that the weird boy who turned out to be a girl gave him on the beach. He grins to himself when he remembers how he was nearly taken in by Vicky's mad idea that the girl was somehow unearthly, an alien. It is obvious to him that the kid was just playing some kind of silly trick on them. Aliens, if there were such things, would not be black for a start, and they definitely would not be female. Then he stops grinning as he remembers how he did not like the kid at all, and how her stuck-up air of being so superior really bugged him. He looks disparagingly at the piece of junk— what did Vicky say about it? That it was a sort of mirror, a mirror for the natives. Natives, huh! Vicky always did have weird ideas!

It can't be a mirror because it's not reflective enough, he thinks, but in the dim light of the stars Michael suddenly has the distinct impression that he can see his face in it for a fraction of a second. Then he seems to be able to see *139* right into the disk itself. It is dark, but a sort of dazzling darkness, like when you close your eyes and look at the sun. Then he jumps and tears his eyes away. He swears out loud. He felt his brain do something with the disk that he had not known it could do. Without thinking twice about it, he hurls the disk away as far as he can. He wants nothing to do with anything so disturbing. He shakes his head like a dog waking from a foolish dream and starts to run up the street.

69 AS MICHAEL crosses the car park in front of the store and runs down the jetty, a figure detaches itself from the shadows where it has been hiding. It watches him get into the waiting boat. The noise of the engine lingers for a long time over the still waters of the gulf.

70 BRENTON and Victoria make their way stealthily toward the beach, going the long way around, because of the rottweiler. By the time they reach the foreshore, Michael, Craig and Craig's dad are far out to sea. But the unknown figure is still there, just putting the finishing touches to the swirly green and orange letters that now decorate the side wall of Penbowie General

Store.

"Ha!" Brenton lets out his breath in a gasp and grabs Victoria's arm, pulling her against the side of the Literary Institute steps. She knocks her head on the railing and says crossly, "What's up?"

"Shhh!" he hisses. "There's someone there, writing on the wall. It's the phantom graffiti artist!"

This on top of the excitement makes his head spin. He doesn't know whether to be shocked or thrilled by the sight of the young man writing nonchalantly and deftly on the wall with an aerosol spray.

Vicky screws up her eyes. "Can you see who it is?"

"No one I know."

The young man steps back and admires his work, laughing lightly under his breath. Then he takes a swift look around the empty street before packing his gear away in a canvas bag. He walks directly toward where Brenton and Victoria are standing in the shadows. He doesn't look in the least apprehensive or alarmed; on the contrary he speaks to them aggressively, confidently. "This is my pitch! Stay off it! I don't want amateurs spoiling my piece."

They see a flash of white teeth as he grins; he turns and looks back at the store. "Big improvement, hey? Brightens up the old dump a bit! Well, see you around, kids!"

He laughs again as he disappears up the street. A few seconds later they hear the sound of an engine start up and a car, unhindered by a muffler, races out of the township along the inland road.

71

"WOW!" Brenton says, starting to laugh too. "Wasn't that something! What a crazy guy!"

"He was breaking the law," Victoria says, though she is also rather elated by the episode. "And what about the shop people? They're not going to be too thrilled. What does it say, anyway? I can't read it from here."

They go a little closer. "Dead N," Brenton reads. DEAD N in the green and orange rap letters, half a meter high, repeated three times over the whitewashed wall.

"What's it mean?" Victoria asks, puzzled.

"I suppose it could mean lots of things. It's like the others, Dead End, Deaden, Dead N. Variations on a theme. N means nuclear," he adds. "Perhaps he's a greenie of some sort."

"Orange and greenie," Vicky starts to reply, but at that moment a dog begins to bark hysterically from the back of the store and a light comes on inside. A window opens.

"Let's go!" Brenton seizes her hand. They dash to the seawall, drop lightly over it and make their way, out of sight from the township up the beach.

72 FROM INLAND comes the long rol-
licking warbling of a magpie, and over
the sea the sky is turning gray. It is nearly dawn. The tide
is full and the children have to pick their way carefully
between the water and the rocks. As they approach the caves
they see something ahead of them. It sees them and waves.

Cal is sitting on a rock, the langscan in her hand. Brenton
and Victoria sit next to her.

"I'm glad you came," she says. "But isn't this usually
sleep time for your species? You are not nocturnal, are you?"

"We are tonight, this morning I should say," Brenton
informs her, but seeing her frown, he adds, "That's just a
joke."

"Ah, a joke," Cal remarks. "Please tell me when you are
joking. One of the most delicate parts of anthropological
studies is the sense of humor of different cultures. The
anthropologist is often told the direct opposite of the truth,
and if she doesn't realize her informant is joking, she can
build up a distorted picture."

"You don't want to get a clear picture of this culture,"
Brenton tells her. "It would drive you mad. We have to
distort it a little to be able to bear it."

Cal does not reply directly to this. "I have been observing
the stars and the tide," she tells them, "and measuring the
length of daylight. It seems it must be around the time of
the shortest night. Do you have a festival for that?"

"I don't think so," Brenton replies, "unless Christmas has
got something to do with it."

"Ah, Christmas," Cal remarks. "I wanted to ask you about that. I heard a lot about it on the radio. Tell me about Christmas."

"Uhh, it's a holiday—people give each other presents, and have a lot of parties, and eat a lot."

"It's a bit more than that!" Victoria interrupts him. Her parents are agnostics, but they admire the ethical teachings of Christ and have tried to impress them on their children. "It's when Jesus Christ was born, that's why it's called Christmas."

"He was a hero?"

"I think he was a bit more than that," she says, wishing she knew more about it, since it is the sort of thing anthropologists like to study. "People think, some people that is, that he was God's son." Cal frowns slightly and Victoria tries to explain. "God is the . . . the spirit that made the world and keeps it all going. Jesus is called the Son of God. He was born on earth as a baby. In a stable," she adds, "and they put him in a manger." She remembers that from Nativity plays at school.

Cal is absorbing this information. "So *God* is what you worship, and Jesus Christ is believed to be God's son?"

"Yeah, but not very many people worship anymore or believe."

"Tell me about God," Cal requests.

Brenton is trying not to laugh. Victoria admits helplessly, "I don't know very much about him."

"But you call God *him*. Therefore you think of God as male?"

Vicky is wondering if this is true. She thinks she might have an idea of what God is, but it's very hard to put into words, and she wouldn't go as far as saying God was male or female—probably a mixture of the two, if she thinks 144 about it, with a fair degree of *itness* thrown in. She wants to please Cal though and give her some anthropologically satisfying details, so she makes an effort to recall the Christian teaching she has heard.

"God created everything," she says finally, "but people messed it up . . ."

"They always do," Brenton puts in.

"Shut up, Brenton! And so Jesus had to come to earth to show people how to stop messing things up and get it right, but they didn't like being told that, so they killed him, by nailing him on a cross. Horrible," she adds, leaning forward and drawing a cross on the sand; it is light enough now to see it. "That's the sign Christians use; you see it everywhere."

"Very interesting," Cal observes. "It is a very ancient symbol."

"Anyway, Jesus didn't stay dead—well, being God, he wouldn't, would he? He came back to life and people that believe in him say he is still alive. That's Easter," she explains.

"Easter?"

"It's another holiday—festival. It's in the autumn here."

Cal nods her head several times as she files all this information away. "But from what I have heard before," she says slowly, "these would be sun-return festivals. You should celebrate them in winter and spring, not now when the sun is about to depart."

"That's because the white people came from the other side of the world," Brenton tells her. "They brought Christmas with them. That's why it's such a muddled setup, winter food, winter decorations, in midsummer. Mad," he adds gloomily, "just like everything else. Peace and goodwill, everyone complains because they've got to eat so much, gets drunk and goes and kills themselves on the roads."

"Are you joking now?" Cal asks him seriously.

"Sort of." Brenton jumps up and swings his arms vigorously across his chest. Where the sky was gray before it is now pearly and pink. "Let's move,' he suggests. "I'm cold."

"I will change back into my other clothes," Cal says, and disappears into the cave. When she comes back Vicky asks, "How're your feet?"

"Not too good," she admits, looking down at them. Where the strap of the thongs has rubbed between her toes the flesh is red and raw. "They are very swollen—I am not used to walking, and I am afraid the cut may be infected. You have organisms here that I have never encountered before and I have no immunity against them. Also the mosquitoes that bit me last night have made me come up in lumps."

She delivers this description of woe quite dispassionately. "It is only to be expected," she tells them, seeing the concerned looks on their faces. "When you visit somewhere primitive you must expect to find the adjustment difficult, even painful." She smiles and nods at them reassuringly, but as they walk back to the jetty their progress is slow.

73

THE JETTY is deserted except for one person fishing off the end of it with a rod and line. It is Wayne Smith, a boy in Brenton's class at school. Wayne has escaped being stunted by radioactive fallout, as Brenton sees it, and is nearly six feet tall. He is also the only Kung Fu expert in Penbowie, and he likes

146 killing things. He has his knife out and he is kneeling over

a large object that thrashes and flaps on the boards of the jetty.

Brenton usually gives Wayne and his cronies a wide berth, but Cal looks at the dying fish and cries out in horror, "What is he doing to it?"

"He's going to kill it."

"But it's so beautiful!"

It is a small Port Jackson shark of subtle coloring and curious design. Forgetting her sore feet, Cal runs down to the end of the pier. With a sigh Brenton commits himself to following her, and Vicky runs with him. By the time they catch up with her she is kneeling beside Wayne.

"Please," she is saying. "Don't kill it." She turns to Brenton. "Tell him not to kill it," she orders.

"Let it go, Wayne," Brenton says casually. "It's no good for eating or bait. You might as well chuck it back."

"I've got to get the bloody hook out," Wayne replies, looking extremely surprised at the interruption to his quiet dawn fishing. "I'm not going to lose that. If I kill the fish I can just cut it out."

The shark flaps again, its gills gaping, its eyes bulging.

"We have to get the hook out," Brenton says to Cal. "If we can get the hook out, he'll let it go."

"I didn't say that," Wayne snorts. "Get out of the way, Trethewan, and take your chocolate frog friend with you."

Brenton is kneeling next to Cal now, his fingers working on the hook. Vicky watches the fish. She can see it is dying. Every time it flaps she thinks it will be the last. The intervals between each flap become longer and longer. The fish is losing its beautiful coloring of brown and copper markings; its eyes are beginning to dull. Still, each time she thinks it has moved for the last time, it surprises her by twitching again.

147

She wonders if it is suffering, if it knows it is going to die, if it knows someone is trying to save it. For Brenton is working doggedly at the hook, shifting it millimeter by millimeter, while Cal is somehow keeping Wayne Smith at bay by force of will.

"Piss off, Trethewan!" Wayne is starting to get ugly, irked by the inexplicable restraint. The hook comes free. Brenton smiles at Cal. The fish flaps feebly between them. Their eyes meet. Brenton lifts the fish, holds it out over the water and lets go. There is a dull splash and then they can all see its dark shape come to life again as it swirls rapidly away.

"Happy now?" Wayne inquires sarcastically. "Done your good deed for the day?"

Cal is looking a little embarrassed. "I am sorry," she says. "I should not have done that. It is not right to interfere in local customs, however barbaric they may appear. I hope I have not offended you in any way."

Wayne stares at her, his jaw dropping. "Are you trying to be funny, kid? And who are you calling barbaric? Bloody nerve!"

"It is a very beautiful life-form," Cal is trying to explain. Brenton pulls on her arm. "Come on," he hisses urgently.

"Yeah, piss off, all of youse," Wayne says again. And because he likes threatening people he shouts after them, "You'd better watch it, Trethewan, because you've got one coming to you!"

74

"WHAT'S Wayne shouting about?" Michael is waiting for them at the end of the jetty, a bucket of assorted fish and squid in his hand. "Look what Craig's dad let me bring home," he goes on without waiting for an answer, showing them his catch. The others regard them rather sadly. They are all quite dead.

"That's the way it goes," Brenton says at last. "You can't save all the beautiful life-forms of the world. You can't even save most of them. Joke," he adds to Cal. "I hope!"

75

AS THEY cross the car park on the foreshore Michael gives a long, surprised whistle. "Heyyy! Look at the store! Oh boy, they'll go ape! I wonder if they've seen it yet. Let's go and ask Danny!"

Brenton and Victoria stare at the writing. In daylight it is even more striking. It's hard to believe they actually saw it being written; the brief encounter now seems like a dream.

Michael is still talking. "It wasn't there when I went past this morning. What time did you come out, Brenton? Did you see anyone? Was it there then?"

"We didn't see a thing, did we, Vicky?"

"Ummm," Vicky replies noncommittally. Michael shoots a glance at her. He's about to pursue the subject **149** when Cal gives a sudden cry and bends down to pick something up out of the gutter.

"You dropped it," she says to Michael, holding the disk out to him.

He backs away. "I threw it away! I don't want it. It's tricky! Just like you, just like Brenton. I don't want to have anything to do with any of your tricks."

"Shut up," Brenton tells him, but he's not really interested in dealing with Michael right now. He's more interested in looking at the disk. "What is it?" he asks, taking it from Cal.

"It's a braingame," she replies. "See if you can play it."

He looks at it and gives a start of surprise as he feels his brain respond to it. His eyes widen as he concentrates deeply. His face is rapt and happy as he stares into it, like someone playing a computer game. "That's fantastic," he says, looking up. "How does it work?"

"You weren't really doing anything with it," Michael butts in. "You're just trying to fool us."

"I suppose you could call it a psychobalancer," Cal says, looking rather anxiously at Michael as she answers Brenton. "We play them a lot to keep our minds in good shape, and to increase our mind power. The more you play with them the greater your abililty."

"Let me have a go," Vicky pleads. She takes the piece of metal and stares into it. "Hey!" she exclaims. "Great! I'm doing it!"

She looks back at Cal, and as their eyes meet she has a clear impression of *something* else, something that cannot be expressed in words, but which she comprehends directly with her whole being. It makes her gulp.

"Very good," Cal says, her eyes flicking away. She is looking pleased with herself, as though she has just conducted a successful experiment.

"What did you do?" Vicky demands suspiciously.

"You were receiving me. You couldn't do it before, but the braingame tuned your mind up sufficiently so that you could."

Vicky feels like a child next to her. She sees her suddenly, and more clearly than ever, as an infinitely more advanced and civilized being. She hands back the disk silently.

Michael feels it too, but his reaction is quite different. "Doesn't she love herself!" he mutters sourly.

"What about the necklace?" Vicky asks. "That feels as though it does something to you too."

"That could be called a bio-balancer. It tunes up your physical self, your body."

"They're real power objects," Brenton marvels, thinking this is better than any fantasy role he's ever played. "Just like magic. Can I keep this onc?"

Cal looks at Michael. "I will give you another one, but this one belongs to Micky."

"I don't want it," he interjects. "I wouldn't take it if you paid me."

This worries Cal even more, though for some time they cannot grasp why. Finally Brenton, after a rather demanding exchange of thought, says slowly, "It's like it's a sort of bad luck not to accept these when they're given to you. I can't explain it very well, our words make it all sound so crude, but it means you're knocking back the person who gives them to you."

"That's just what I am doing," Michael says. "Because I don't like people making a fool of me. I don't want my brain tuned up; I'm very happy with it the way it is. At least dumb weirdos can't take me in."

He stands still as the others start to walk on, and after a few moments shouts after them, "You're all crazy. I'm going back to Danny's."

AT THE CENTER

CHRIS greets the two children and Cal from the paddock. "I woke up this morning and the house was empty. Where've you all been? And where's Mick?"

"We've just been down to the beach," Brenton replies. "Mick's gone to Danny's. Someone's painted the side of the shop—the same sort of thing as at the hospital and the pool, and Mick's gone to get all the latest info."

The three of them stand and watch Chris as she approaches the fence. They are all thinking different things. Brenton is wondering if she is still mad at him. Victoria is noticing that she has again assumed her magical look. And Cal . . . but no one can tell what Cal is thinking behind her smooth dark skin and unreadable black eyes.

"How infuriating for them," Chris remarks. "I hope they pick up whoever it is soon. I think it's unforgivable that these hooligans come out from the city and vandalize our property." She puts her hand up to shield her eyes from the early morning sun and smiles at the three of them. "Bathsheba had her kids in the night. Come and see them."

The mother goat swings her head around and stares at the visitors with her proud yellow eyes. The two little ones, slightly wobbly on their rubbery hoofs, peer out from behind her. Cal is delighted with them. "Beautiful!" she exclaims.

"They're rather cute, aren't they," Chris replies. Hardly **155** pausing, she goes on. "Unfortunately they're both boys. I'm not sure what we're going to do with them."

"What do you mean?" Cal asks.

"We can't afford to keep them as pets," Chris explains. "They're meant to be a moneymaking venture. I'm hoping to be able to sell the young ones, but most people want females. We really should use them for meat." She can't quite bring herself to say *eat them*. "It makes the most sense."

Cal is puzzling this one out as they walk back to the house. The Burmese cat, Tang, jumps off the veranda roof and rolls over on his back for Brenton to scratch his belly.

"This is a male, isn't he?" Cal says, "but you will not eat him?"

"Eat a cat!" Chris exclaims. "What a revolting idea!"

"Cats are pets," Brenton tells Cal. "No one eats pets. But goats are not quite pets—so it's OK to eat them. But I'm not going to," he adds, glancing firmly at his mother. She, always busy, has walked on ahead and is no longer listening to them.

2

"DID YOU ever hear of a tribe called the Narrangga?" Vicky asks Chris later in the day. The children are decorating the family room with paper chains and fake snow, while Chris works on Shelley's dress.

"Why do you want to know?" she replies. "Is your friend related to them in some way?"

There is a moment's silence while they all look at Cal.

"Only very remotely," she says. "But I would like to know more about them."

"We've got a little booklet on them somewhere," Chris says. "Have a look on the bookshelf in the hall, Brenton. It's got a yellow cover, I seem to remember. I bought it at the museum. . . ." She is frowning as she tries to remember something else. "There were some remains down on the shore, in the dunes where the caravan park is now. Someone came from the city, oh it must be ten years ago, and got very excited about them. But before anyone could do anything about them it was all bulldozed by mistake to make a playground."

That, and the slimness of the booklet, make Brenton and Victoria feel extremely sad.

"Forty thousand years of living here," Brenton says to Cal, "and so little of it remains. I wish I knew more about them now. I wish we still knew how they lived."

Cal nods in agreement. "The things that made their society rich cannot be recorded by your society—you simply do not have the means or the approach."

"The name's almost the same as Narringa, the tracking station," Brenton remarks, skimming through the book. "The one where all the protests have been."

It's even more ironic than he thinks at first. He stops at random and reads a few lines. "Hey, listen to this. 'Being cut off from other tribes very little was known of war, consequently their weapons were few.' "

The contrast between the two societies who have inhabited the same physical space hits him painfully. He looks at Cal and knows that, despite her professional dispassionate approach, she feels it too.

3 THE FOLLOWING day is Christmas Eve. Victoria wakes up feeling oppressed and fearful. By the afternoon the feeling has localized itself in the pit of her stomach and turned itself into pain. Later she realizes it's the start of her first period. She gazes in surprise at the rusty-colored blood. She knows all about menstruation, has known for years, but she's rather astonished that it should actually happen to her. And it seems to have come out of the blue; she doesn't feel any more grown-up, any closer to womanhood, than she did a few weeks ago. She hasn't got any of the right things, and it's too late to go to the shops. She spends a few minutes wishing acutely that her mother were here, and then wanders down the passage to Shelley's room.

Shelley is leaning forward, peering into her mirror. "Hi, Vicky! Come in! My nose is peeling, isn't that terrible? Just before Christmas, too!"

"It doesn't show." Vicky comes up to the dressing table and looks at the bottles and tubes of makeup. Shelley pats cover-up cream gently on her nose. "Did you want something?" she asks.

"I think my periods have started. I haven't got any of the right things."

Shelley drops the tube of cream and jumps up. She gives Vicky a hug. "Congratulations! That's really exciting!"

"It is?" Vicky looks at her bewildered.

"Sure is! It means you're growing up. You'll be having **158** boyfriends next!" She giggles to herself, and the warm, half-suppressed feeling of excitement that she has been exuding all week bubbles out more strongly. "I'll get you the things you need. Have you got any pain?"

"A little," Vicky admits.

"I'll give you one of my tablets; they're brilliant."

When Vicky is fixed up with all she needs, and the pain-killer is starting to work, Shelley has another idea. "I think we should celebrate," she announces. "Have you ever tasted champagne? I'm going to get you a glass." She gives Vicky another hug. "It's so great having you here, Vicky, it's just like having a little sister. I've always wanted one; you know how dreadful younger brothers are!"

When she comes back with the champagne she is more elated than ever. "Dad won't notice one bottle missing," she chuckles. "We're going to have a little girls-only party."

She makes Victoria sit down at the dressing table. "Now," she commands. "Sit still, I'm going to put some makeup on you."

Vicky takes a sip of the icy, sparkling, straw-colored drink. It prickles her nose like tears. She doesn't particularly like it, but she likes the idea of sitting there drinking it, and she feels a rush of gratitude and affection for Shelley. Under the makeup her face feels slightly heavy and unfamiliar, as though she has after all become a new person and has crossed some sort of boundary between childhood and adult-hood.

"Gee, you've got lovely skin, Vicky," Shelley observes. "I bet your nose never peels! There, look at yourself. How do you like that?"

Her face stares back at her, mature and *pretty*.

4 CHRISTMAS comes, heralded by angels on the radio and hangovers in the house. Presents are exchanged. Victoria has brought unusual gifts from Kano market, a carved Arabian dagger for Brenton, a native bow with allegedly poisoned arrows for Michael and silver bangles for Chris and Shelley. In exchange the family gives her a bulky parcel, which, when she unwraps it, makes her gasp with pleasure. It is the finished wall hanging, its blue, green and gold colors now completed and perfect.

"You can take it to boarding school with you, Vicky," Chris tells her. "It'll remind you of home." She hears what she has said and smiles at the girl. "Of *here*, I should say. But I really do feel as if you're part of the family now."

As Vicky smiles back at her, she realizes, rather to her surprise, that she is starting to feel it too. It means that the mention of school gives her even more of an unpleasant jolt. It's still far away in the future, but she knows suddenly she's going to have to think about it before too long, and she's not sure she wants to.

Geoff has been doing something secret in the kitchen while the present unwrapping ceremony takes place and now he calls out, "Come in here, love. I've got a surprise for you!"

It is a brand-new, shining dishwasher. Chris is bowled over by it. "You really shouldn't have," she keeps saying. "We can't afford it."

"Isn't it fantastic," Shelley squeals. "Didn't you guess,

Mum? I think it's such a great present. No more fighting over the washing up!"

Brenton is unwrapping a parcel which says on it TO BRENTON FROM BRENTON. He takes out a smart new diving mask. "Very nice," he says. "Just what I wanted, thank you very much."

"Here's something else for you, you maniac," Michael says, tossing over a package wrapped in Rawlings' plain brown paper. Brenton looks at him in surprise. "You weren't supposed to get me anything," he remarks. "I haven't got anything for you."

"That just goes to show that I'm much nicer than you," Michael rejoins smugly. He is grinning as Brenton takes off the wrapping paper. Two aerosol cans tumble out; one lid is green, the other orange.

"Oh, very tricky!"

"That's for your next job," Michael says wickedly. "I thought you might be running short."

Brenton gives him a curious look and decides on the spur of the moment to go along with the trick.

"Thanks a lot!" he enthuses. "Doing the shop did leave me a bit low. And I've got another site all picked out. Now I can get on with it." He is weighing the cans in his hands, and an image of the new galvanized fence in front of the shack flashes across his mind. His eyes gleam as he lets himself imagine what it would feel like to stand out there in the dark and paint on it in orange and green.

He comes out of his dream to hear his father demand sharply, "What are you two clowns on about now?"

"They're just joking, Dad," Shelley states firmly. "Don't take any notice of them." She glares at Michael. "It's not very funny!"

"I'm not joking," Michael assures her. "Danny saw Bren-   **161** ton outside the shop the night it was painted. He knows something about it."

"If I find out you're involved in that sort of vandalism, I'll tear you limb from limb," Geoff tells Brenton angrily. He would have said more, but Chris is calling to him from the kitchen.

"We must get organized for the meal. People will be arriving soon."

THE WAY OUT

1 LATE ON Christmas afternoon the sea has returned silently and unobtrusively. It gently covers rocks and boulders, laps the foot of the cliff, lifts the fishnet and holds it upright. Millimeter by millimeter it deepens. It is deep enough to wade in, deep enough to swim in. Deep enough to drown in.

The woman is sitting at the table in the shack, a sheaf of newspaper cuttings in her hand. She does not need to read them; she knows them all by heart. On the table flies buzz around the half-eaten Christmas feast. She gets up, takes a can of insecticide and sprays them. The fumes make her cough; lighting a cigarette she goes outside.

Inside the shack dying flies buzz on their backs in vain.

The woman stands on the cliff's edge, her mind full of fear and dead children, full of headlines and television images that have become part of her. She looks down on the rising sea, face hard, heart twisting.

2 AT THE Trethewans' the Christmas feast is mostly finished, but the veranda is full of large people, friends and relations, relaxing with drinks, bowls of nuts, glacé fruit and chocolates.

"Brenton!" his mother calls him as he's disappearing into his room to get on with the *Labyrinth*, "have you seen Vicky?"

"No." He would have left it there, but she continues, "Do check up on her and see if she's all right."

"Okay," he says and crosses the passageway to her room.

"Mum wants to know if you're all right," he says as he opens the door.

"Yes, I'm all right, I suppose," Vicky replies, carefully not looking up at him. "I'm just not sure what I should be doing."

"What you should be doing? What do you mean?"

"Well, should I be helping your mother, or talking to the visitors, or keeping out of the way?"

Brenton looks at her in surprise. "What do you want to do?"

"I don't want to do any of them, that's the problem," she says, without meaning to. "I don't want to be here at all." The feeling that she was getting to be part of the family has been chased away by the invasion of visitors, all strangers to her.

Brenton says awkwardly, "I suppose it's a bit rough being away from your family at Christmas."

166 "Yes, but don't feel sorry for me, otherwise I'll probably

start crying and I'm trying not to." She laughs rather feebly and takes a deep breath.

"I'd feel sorry for anyone landed with this family," he remarks. "What was your crime? You must have done something terrible."

"It's not your family," she replies almost indignantly. "You've got a terrific family. You've all been really kind to me." She stops and blinks suspiciously. "Oh, I don't want to talk about it, Brenton. There's nothing I can do to change any of it, and talking about it only makes me feel worse."

"Well, let's go down to the beach," he suggests. "We can tell Cal all about Christmas Day in Australia—that should give her some interesting patterns to observe—and I can try out my new mask."

"Okay, but I don't think I'd better swim," Vicky says, very conscious of her new status.

"You don't have to swim. You can stand on the beach, collect shells, talk to Cal, whatever you like. At least you won't be moping around here feeling sorry for yourself. Give Mick a shout; he'll probably want to come too."

3 THE SEA has gone an evening color of purple, and through it the fishnet cuts like a wire fence. The wind and the flow of the tide are pulling the boys toward it. Victoria's eyes have been following them, as she crouches on the one tiny patch of sand left, looking for shells.

In between one glance and the next, one of the heads has disappeared.

167

Brenton dives to follow a school of fish, marveling at their sleek transparent bodies, a shade between silver and milk, and their dark, oily eyes. He accompanies them, imagining himself a fish, not a shark or some other predator, but one of them. He turns when they turn, darts when they dart, but, he is thinking, I can never get to know what they're really like, because what they're doing now they only do because I'm here.

He lets the water flow in and out of his mouth. He can almost believe he has gills and could stay under forever.

The net floats alongside his body. It touches his shoulder like a caress. Instinctively he turns his head toward it, forgetting the breathing tube by his right ear. The snorkel slips easily through the mesh and hooks itself neatly to the other side.

Brenton experiences one moment of pure panic as he struggles against the net, thereby enmeshing the tube further. He gasps and bubbles burst out and float upward.

Oh hell! he is thinking. What a dumb, bloody thing to do. I can't leave the mask here. But he can't dislodge the snorkel and his breath is running out. Desperately he pulls the mask off his head and surfaces.

He breathes deeply and is preparing to dive again when he hears shouting; he squints against the sunset to the beach.

Pam is standing on the water's edge, her face contorted with rage and fear. She is shouting, "Get away from the net, you bloody little idiot. Get away from the frigging net."

Michael approaches Brenton with his fast, showy crawl. "What's up?"

"Lost the mask. It's caught in the net."

"Oh, nice one! You want me to dive for it?"

168 "I can do it," Brenton replies and dives again.

Pam is knee-deep in the water now. "Get away from the net, you little dickheads!"

Victoria watches and listens amazed. She has never heard an adult swear at a child in this fashion. She has always thought of adults as essentially benign. This one seems to be of an entirely different species, definitely a hostile one. The gulf between childhood and adulthood has never seemed so vast. And Victoria knows that she has already been launched across it; there is no way she can stop in midair and go back, though right now she desperately wants to.

Brenton surfaces again empty-handed and catches another volley of swearing.

"What's she going on about?" he says to Michael.

"She's telling us to stay away from the net."

"I can't leave the mask there!" Brenton dives again.

Victoria's instinct is to escape from the woman, but she doesn't want to abandon the boys, and now the situation is complicated further by the arrival of Cal. She is limping slightly as she approaches Vicky and there is an indefinable air about her of things not being quite as they should be.

Vicky looks at her curiously. "Is something wrong?"

Cal smiles back cheerfully enough, but as she takes another step forward she winces slightly. "My feet hurt a little," she admits. "I have never walked so much in my life."

Brenton has surfaced again. The water pours off his sleek, dark hair and thick black lashes. "I can't get it loose," he gasps to Michael.

"I'll have a go, I'll be able to see better."

"Take your snorkel off then."

Michael is trying to detach the breathing tube from the mask when the woman shouts again.

"Shark! Shark!"

Both boys turn at this. A woman died in a shark attack **169** last summer. Sharks are a real danger, though a remote one. Neither of them can see the ominous triangular fin, but the strengthening wind has whipped the sea up into choppy waves that they cannot quite see over.

"We'd better go in," Michael says.

Brenton swears again. They turn and swim fast to the shore.

Her face is very close to theirs, thin and hard. Another torrent of abuse pours from her mouth.

Brenton tries to explain. "Sorry. I got my mask caught . . ."

She does not want to listen. "I told you not to swim there! You could have been drowned, you little idiots!"

It's as though she is finding a deep and savage pleasure in seeing her anxieties justified. Brenton feels she would have liked him to drown or be taken by a shark; it would vindicate her in some way. He is angry enough already at losing the mask. He doesn't like being sworn at.

"Ah, get stuffed!" he says loudly.

"Don't you swear at me, you little creep. I'm just trying to stop you killing yourself."

"Come on, Brenton," Michael urges. "We'll get the mask loose at low tide. We'll come back later."

Pam follows them out of the water, still muttering bitterly, and then she sees Victoria and Cal. Her eyes narrow as a new line of attack occurs to her.

"Tell that black kid I'm going to the police about her," she says loudly to Victoria. She doesn't address Cal even though she is standing close to her. She talks across her as though she is invisible or an idiot. "I've checked the caravan park, and no one's ever heard of her there. That means she must be camping out on the beach. That's not allowed.

170 And it's dangerous."

"She's not camping on the beach anymore," Brenton replies. "She's staying with us." He gives the woman a defiant stare. "We'll take the cliff path, if you don't mind."

"I don't mind you using it," she exclaims loudly. "I just don't want you to do anything stupid and get yourselves into trouble. As long as the dog's on the chain you're welcome to go through this way."

But her eyes, as she follows them, are hard and angry, and she is still quivering with rage. When they are crossing the yard she says sharply to Cal, "What's wrong with your foot, love?"

"I am not sure," Cal replies. "Nothing serious, I hope."

"Mum can check it out," Brenton adds.

"I don't like the look of it," Pam says. "It could be infected. Could turn quite nasty. Tell your mum we'll be up in a little while. And see if you can stay out of trouble for the rest of the day."

4 "COW!" Brenton swears expressively as they cross the road and start walking slowly up the driveway.

"Why do we make her so angry?" Cal inquires, puzzled.

"She's a bit mad," Michael remarks shortly. Victoria notices he doesn't look directly at Cal either, as though her dark skin in some way makes her invisible to him too.

"The trouble is, she's sure to tell Dad," Brenton says with a feeling of doom. "Mum invited them up for drinks this evening."

"You shouldn't have sworn at her," Michael points out. **171**

"She shouldn't have sworn at me!" Brenton retorts righteously.

"Why do people swear?" Cal asks. "And aren't the adults meant to look after the children?"

"She was looking after them in a way," Victoria explains. "She was trying to stop anything bad happening to them. It's just that her way of doing it is so unpleasant."

"You don't know if she wants something terrible to happen to you or not," Brenton agrees. "If it did happen, she'd be glad. It would prove her right. How's your foot?" he continues, as Cal stumbles over a stone.

"It's hurting," she admits, with an air of surprise that it should.

"We'll fix it up when we get home," he assures her protectively.

"She's not really going to stay with us, is she?" Michael demands. "Dad'll throw a fit."

"What would the Narrangga have done?" Brenton asks Cal curiously. "Would they have just accepted you as one of them?"

"I don't know," Cal admits. "Possibly, possibly not."

"Our society is so complicated," Brenton groans. "Everyone fits in their own little place, and there's no room for strangers."

"Don't worry," Cal reassures him. "My society is far more complex and infinitely more structured."

"But what would you do with a stray space traveler if they turned up on your doorstep."

"We do not have doorsteps," Cal replies seriously.

Michael makes an expression of disbelief. "Brenton, you idiot, this is not a space traveler. It's a stray kid who I think had better stray back to wherever she came from." But he **172** still does not look straight at Cal.

By this time they have nearly reached the house. "We've got to do something with her," Victoria says. "If your parents won't let her stay inside, we'll have to hide her somewhere."

"We could put her in the shed," Brenton replies. "We'll make a hiding place behind the straw."

"Count me out," Michael interrupts. "I don't want to have anything to do with it."

"You don't have to have anything to do with it. Just don't give us away!"

The brothers' eyes meet and lock. Michael's are mutinous and doubtful, Brenton's urgent, forceful. Michael looks away. "OK," he mutters.

5 THE SHED is full of objects, ranging from the abandoned and cobwebby to the new and well-maintained. A history of the whole family could be found there if anyone had the time and patience to sift through them. As each piece of gear has been outgrown it has been stored away in the shed. If you dug deep enough you would find a playpen and a baby walker buried for twelve years. Nearer the top are training wheels and wading pools, inflatable toys for swimming, junior-sized masks and flippers, tennis rackets without strings, deflated footballs. All these artifacts of the late twentieth century are piled on wide shelves that cover one side of the shed. Across the end closest to the door is Geoff's workbench, arranged meticulously with tools hanging in rows of descending size, and overhead the power tools, saw, drill and sander, strictly forbidden to the boys.

Across the other end, bales of straw and hay for the animals are stored, and down the opposite side stand the fodder bins. Brenton takes the inspection lamp from the workbench and switches it on. Its brilliant beam sends shadows jumping around the shed. He shines it in Victoria's face. "Ve haff vays of making you talk!" he says menacingly. "Ve belieff you haff somevun hiding herein!" Victoria flinches away, and Brenton swings the beam around, flashing it down behind the bales. "Aha! So!" he says in triumph.

Victoria peers in. There is a narrow space between the bales and the wall, just big enough for someone to hide in. She nods her head a little doubtfully. "Do you think she'll be OK?"

"She can't stay in the cave anymore," Brenton says in his own voice. "We'll get a rug and some pillows."

6 CAL IS standing by the goats' fence watching them feed. They throw their sleek brown heads up from time to time and look at her nervously, rolling their bold yellow eyes. She stares at them fixedly, catches the eyes of a young doe and holds the gaze, until the animal snorts, drops her head and moves anxiously away.

Tang watches this from the top of a fence post. His head is held low and he snakes his neck slightly in the direction of the girl. He gives a low yowl. Cal turns and looks at him. There is the same instant of a gaze held and some unspoken communication between girl and animal. The hairs rise along Tang's back and he growls, retreating a little.

The noise of an approaching vehicle makes Brenton and Victoria jump.

"Quick!" Brenton's voice is urgent.

From the shed door they call to Cal.

"Cal! Cal, come here! Hurry!"

She walks unhurriedly toward them. The yellow Toyota from the shack is coming up the drive.

"Damn!" Brenton swears and, pulling on Cal's arm, hustles her into the shed.

"Stay behind here," he instructs her, showing the hiding place behind the straw. "Don't let anyone see you. You've got to hide for a bit. That woman's getting suspicious. She'll start making trouble for us; she might even go to the police, and then we'll have to try and explain where you've come from . . . !"

"No, no," Cal whispers. "That would be wrong. No one must know. I must leave if that is going to happen."

"That's why we've got to hide you. Now, I'm going to get you some blankets."

7 BRENTON is hoping to get into the house unobserved and then get out to the shed again, but he is waylaid by his mother in the kitchen and despite intense protest forced to help her carry trays of drinks and snacks out onto the veranda.

The adults have been drinking heavily most of the day, and by now their faces are flushed and their voices loud. Brenton looks from one to the other with his stern, fourteen-year-old eyes. It irritates him immensely that Shelley and **175**

Jason are part of the group, both smoking and drinking. His father is telling a joke he has heard a dozen times before. It must be programmed in, he thinks bitterly, to be told at the twentieth beer.

"And what do you think she said?" Geoff is laughing immoderately in anticipation of the punch line. He is laughing so much that for a few seconds he cannot speak at all, and Brenton, putting down the tray on the coffee table, can't resist saying it for him.

"Oh, you poor thing, I've had tennis elbow!"

He says it in a weary, singsong voice that completely destroys whatever vestige of humor the joke might have had.

It's a mistake to draw attention to himself. Not only does his father glare at him, but Pam, who has joined the group with her husband, also fixes him with her hard eyes.

"Too bad about your mask," she says into the silence. "Teach you to listen next time, won't it?"

"What's that?" his father asks immediately.

"The boy lost his mask in the net," Pam replies, taking a swig of her drink. "Still, he was OK, that's the main thing, isn't it?"

You cow, Brenton is thinking, but he says nothing and turns to walk away. His father's voice stops him. "Just a minute, son. Come back here."

"I can hear you from here," Brenton says, turning around, not wanting to get too close to the angry red face and the large red hands.

"Up here!" Geoff beckons with one finger.

Geez! Brenton thinks. He's going to play the heavy father, because he's got an audience. Brenton's not sure if it's worse to take whatever's coming now, or to cut and run for it, postponing punishment till later. But running away suddenly seems impossibly childish. He might have done it six months ago. Now he cannot. He moves a little closer, wary and defiant.

"You went swimming down by the net?"

"Yeah."

"So where's your new mask?"

"It got caught in the net. I'll go and get it at low tide." There's a chance his father will not take it all too seriously. It depends on how much he has had to drink. If he has had just enough to make him cheerful, it will be all right, but if he's had a lot it makes him belligerent. Brenton risks a smile and says, "I'm sorry."

It is the wrong thing to say. "I'll teach you to be sorry," his father shouts furiously. His arm shoots up very quickly and Brenton gets a swift smack on the ear. It is a heavy one; it jars his teeth and makes him reel.

"That's the way, Geoff," someone laughs. "Show 'em who's boss!"

Brenton rubs the side of his face. It stings enough to make his eyes water, but the pain is nothing compared to the humiliation. Being hit is bad enough, but being hit in front of people is unbearable.

"Just don't want anything to happen to you kids," Pam says. "You don't know how precious they are till you lose them," she adds, looking around the circle of faces.

An awkward silence follows, mostly but not entirely sympathetic; it is broken a few seconds later by someone throwing in a comment with a laugh. "I hear they decorated your hospital for you, Geoff."

Geoff is staring after his son as he walks away. "Yeah," he says. "If I get my hands on the bugger I'll crucify him."

8 BRENTON opens the door of the house. It is quiet, cool and familiar but it fails to soothe him. His mother is in the kitchen, preparing yet another tray of snacks.

"For heaven's sake," he says angrily. "You're not giving them more food? Hasn't everyone filled their faces enough?"

"What's wrong with you? Aren't you having a nice day?"

"I'm having a bloody awful day, since you ask."

Chris is tired and edgy and has had a little too much to drink herself. "I don't know what your problem is, Brenton," she explodes at him. "You get everything you could possibly want and you're still not satisfied. I work and work to try and make it a happy day for everyone, and you spoil things by being bad tempered. Well, I'm fed up with it. If you can't enjoy yourself like a normal person, you can get out. Go on, disappear! Go and mope somewhere else."

Like a normal person? he is thinking. Is this what normal people do? How on earth am I going to cope with growing up like a normal person in a world I don't want to have anything to do with?

He gives her a resigned look and leaves the room. A small brown shape detaches itself from the shadows and walks after him. When he gets to his room he picks Tang up and lies down on his bed. The cat curls up on his chest and begins to purr. Brenton lies there for a long time, stroking the cat and looking at the mushroom clouds on the wall.

9 MUCH LATER when, finally, the laughter and the jokes have died away, the last car has departed erratically and noisily down the drive and the house is dark and silent, Brenton still cannot sleep. Too many things are battling it out inside his head.

He gets out of bed, past Michael, who is dead to the world, and goes to the kitchen. As he passes his parents' bedroom door, he hears their voices.

"He worries me." That is his mother. Is she talking about him? "I sometimes wonder if he's really all right."

His father says something he cannot hear. He must be in bed, but his mother would be sitting at the dressing table, removing her makeup. Her voice is pitched so it will reach across the room. Brenton hears her continue, "Suppose it's schizophrenia. That suddenly occurs in teenagers."

Schizophrenia! he thinks. I hope she's not referring to me. He feels quite insulted by the idea. Schizophrenia indeed! The whole of society is schizophrenic, not him!

"Don't worry about him, he's perfectly normal."

"Thanks, Dad," Brenton tells him silently.

"He's just stupid," his father goes on.

"Huh!" Brenton decides he's had enough of this midnight eavesdropping. He will go out to the shed and make sure Cal is all right. He stops by the kitchen to take a jug of water from the fridge and collects a couple of glasses from the cupboard. The dishwasher is swirling gently to itself as he lets himself quietly out of the house.

10

CAL IS AWAKE. She takes the water gratefully and drinks deeply. "Brenton," she whispers. "I need my things. They are still in the cave. I daren't spend any more time without my clothes, and I will need the photosynthesizer as soon as the sun comes up again. Can you get them for me? I would go myself, but my feet hurt very much tonight and I do not think I can walk that far."

He looks at his watch. It is twelve-thirty. "Yeah, OK," he agrees. "If I go now I might be able to get my mask. The tide will be out." He takes the flashlight from the hook on the wall and slips on an old pair of thongs that someone has abandoned under the workbench. "I'll be back soon," he promises.

11

BRENTON pads quietly down the driveway and along the road to the township. A couple of cars pass him, tooting a Christmas greeting; otherwise there is no one around. No one on the jetty either, or the beach. Lighting the flashlight he picks his way carefully between the rocks and pools. The night is mild and still, with the unnatural stillness that sometimes precedes a storm. He feels he can taste rain in the air, very distant, but coming. A thin moon is lying on its back, the old moon in its arms, both heavy with moisture. When the south-westerlies drive up the coast the beach at night smells fresh and alive, but this night it smells of death and rot. Unwillingly he thinks of Brett and the other boy and of all the people who have ever drowned at sea. He seems to see their white faces and their desperate eyes at his feet.

He quickens his pace, as if he is running away from something. But he can't escape his thoughts of Brett and his mother and the crazy, malicious turn her grief has taken. He wonders if she hates him for being alive when Brett is dead. He thinks again that if, if only, he had gone with the boys they would still be alive.

Despite the warm night, he shivers; such a narrow band of coincidence separates life and death; such heedless and insignificant choices turn out to be the wrong ones—turn out to be the dead end.

Jogging over the rocks, his skin tingles as he thinks about the graffiti. Uncanny that they should be on this theme too, as though they had been written for him. He considers their message again. Tiredness and anxiety are making him see mysterious connections where possibly there are none. He thinks about the N, the DEAD N. The *n* in their names which distinguishes Brett from Brent. Could Dead N be the difference between Brett and Brenton? He wishes he could see the phantom graffiti artist again and ask him what he means.

The cave looms ahead. Brenton shines the flashlight around it, but Cal's pack is so well camouflaged he has to kneel and feel around with his fingers before he locates it.

For a moment he crouches in the cave, the flashlight out, the pack under his arm. He can sense the whole weight of the cliff above him. He wonders fleetingly what it would be like to be buried alive. Worse than drowning? Worse *181* than a car wreck? But possibly better than radiation sickness or heat flash.

Now for the mask. As he approaches the cliff path he can see the net lying lifeless on the sand. It's too heavy for him to lift, so he goes along it on his knees, feeling for the hard, black rubber. Once his fingers encounter a half-dead fish, which makes him jump by giving a convulsive flap.

"Sorry, life-form," he whispers to it. "There's nothing I can do for you."

The snorkel is entangled about halfway along the net. It's hard to believe the water was over his head right here. Using the flashlight he gets it loose, picks up Cal's pack again, tucks both mask and pack under his arm and stands up.

And sways. He is shivering more than ever. Suddenly he is completely, utterly exhausted. His bed has never seemed so inviting, or so far away. He knows he simply cannot walk all the way back through the township again. He takes the path up the cliff.

Of course, the rottweiler practically ruptures itself barking at him, and of course the lights flash on in the shack. He knows she's watching him as he stumbles across the yard and scales the wall, but he's too tired to care. He looks back from the top of the wall. Pam is standing in the doorway, one hand on the dog's head, looking after him, staring as if she saw a ghost. Perhaps she wishes she did. Their glances lock across the dimly lit space between them. "I just came back for the mask," Brenton says lamely, waving it at her. And then, because she looks so disturbingly sad standing there, he adds awkwardly, "I'm sorry."

He can't tell if she's heard him or not. She makes a gesture with her hand that could be a wave, or it could be a shake of the fist; it's hard to tell. She takes a step backward into the darkness and shuts the door with a slam.

Brenton scrapes the inside of his thigh sliding off the wall and swears.

12

"I THINK I might go with Dad on this race today," Chris tells Shelley the morning after Christmas. "I'm feeling really strung out. I'd like to get away for a couple of days."

"Why not?" Shelley agrees cheerfully, pouring coffee from the percolator. "Jason and I will look after the kids. It'll do you good."

"Are you sure you can manage?"

"Of course we can! What could go wrong? Mick could go to Danny's for the night, Brenton looks after himself and Vicky's no trouble at all. She's so sensible."

Chris nods in agreement to this, wondering at the same time if it's really healthy for Vicky to be always so well behaved, and privately wishing the girl would be a little more relaxed. "It's Brenton that worries me most," she says aloud, thinking of the previous day's disasters.

"Oh, Mum, Brenton's OK!"

"Thank you!" Brenton has just come into the room. "It's nice to know I've got my fans. Can I ask why you're discussing me?"

"If I go with Dad on the race today, will you promise to behave yourself?"

"Mum!" He looks at her in disgust. "I'm not six years old, you know!"

"You really act like it sometimes. What about yesterday? Losing your new mask, quite apart from nearly getting yourself drowned."

183

He screws up his face in exasperation. "I got the mask back last night. And there was never any real danger—she just makes an awful fuss about things."

"Well, I was very disappointed to hear that you swore at her."

"Swore at her! Mum, you should have heard what she said to us. What I said was positively polite. Ask Vicky, she heard it all."

Victoria has just come into the kitchen after feeding the animals and is washing her hands at the sink. She discovers to her surprise that she wants to stand up for Brenton, whether he is right or not. Without stopping to analyze this new feeling she says fiercely, "She was really rude to Brenton and Mick, even before they said anything. She didn't need to shout at them; she only had to tell them. I don't think adults should swear at children," she adds righteously. "And she was horrible to Cal."

Chris makes an understanding face. "It's true, she's not the easiest of people. Even before Brett died she was pretty hard to get on with. You'd better stay away from that part of the beach for the next few days."

"Jason can take us over to Barbridge," Brenton suggests. "The swimming's much better there anyway."

"Shelley can use the Falcon in the daytime," Chris says. "As long as you're really careful, Shell, and remember . . ."

"Don't drink and drive!" they all chime in together.

"You might spill some," Brenton adds.

"As if I would!" Shelley exclaims.

"Dad does," Brenton says. "So does everyone we know."

"That's different," Chris says. "They're experienced drivers."

"Bullsh . . ." Brenton starts to say, but he catches Shelley's eye and closes his mouth. It's just one more instance of adults saying one thing and doing another, of rules that everybody agrees ought to be kept but nobody wants to keep themselves.

"And you think I'm schizophrenic!" he accuses his mother.

"Did you hear that?" she replies, rather put out. "What were you doing, creeping around the house in the middle of the night, listening at keyholes?"

"I told you, I went to look for my mask. I couldn't help hearing you—you were talking loud enough." Brenton has taken the dice out of his pocket and is fiddling nervously with them. "You don't really think I am, do you?"

He would like her to deny it immediately, but she doesn't. Instead she reaches for a cigarette and after lighting it says, "You have been behaving in a strange way lately."

"I'm the normal one," he replies aggressively. "I think you're the one with problems. It's definitely abnormal to sit around here celebrating Christmas and making wall hangings while the world goes crazy."

"Oh Brenton!" his mother replies. "I can't put the world to rights. I just get on with my own life as best I can."

He is wondering if this is really good enough. "Your parents must have thought about this," he says to Vicky. "And they went off to help other people, didn't they?"

"If we went off to help other people there'd be nowhere for Vicky to go," Shelley points out, exchanging glances with her mother in a sort of humorous and rueful sisterhood that also includes Victoria. Brenton regards them almost enviously. He knows no such fellowship with anyone— except a small dark alien of uncertain age, race and sex.

Shelley starts to clear the table, opening the new dishwasher and stacking the breakfast dishes in it. "Beautiful, isn't it? Weren't you thrilled with your present, Mum?"

"I'll say! It doesn't argue or answer back, just gets on with the job. I wish I could say the same for you," she adds, looking at Brenton. She is tired, a little hung over and irritable. The letdown after all the busy preparations for Christmas is beginning to hit her. Brenton has made her feel guilty as he always does . . . but what can any one person do? A couple of days sailing will be just the thing, she decides; she will be able to get away from everything and relax.

"We'll be back tomorrow night. I don't suppose you can get into too much trouble in that time."

13

THERE IS a frantic rush to get things ready. When Chris comes outside to start loading up the Falcon, Cal is kneeling by the herb garden examining the plants.

"I wanted to ask you," she says seriously to Chris, "about your plants. What do you use them for and how do you grow them?"

"Well, not now, dear!" Chris laughs to mask her annoyance. "I'm just getting ready to go away. I'll tell you some other time." She is frowning as she speaks as though she is trying to remember something else. Cal is watching her closely and intensely. Chris shakes her head abruptly and returns to her work, and when they are all ready to leave Cal gets in the car with the children. Nobody says anything about her being there, nobody asks her what she is doing.

186   Geoff is already at the mooring off Farborough. Chris

kisses the children good-bye, managing to look both worried and relieved at the same time. They stand on the quay and wave as the dinghy reaches the yacht and then wave again as the graceful boat gets under way to join the flotilla of others out near the horizon.

14 ON THE yacht Chris exclaims with annoyance. "I've just remembered something," she tells Geoff. "I didn't want that strange kid hanging around while we're away and I forgot to say anything."

"Don't worry about it," he replies, his face tense with expectation for the race ahead. "Nothing's going to go wrong."

15 "I'M STARVING," Mick announces. "Let's get a hamburger, Shelley."

As keeper of the housekeeping money she makes a quick calculation and decides they can afford it. "Where do you want to go?"

"We might as well go to the pool, since we're here anyway. Then we can swim later, too."

At the pool they split up into groups. Michael and Shelley both have friends they go to sit with. Brenton, Victoria and Cal sit together, outsiders, watching.

"What have you been up to?" Brenton asks Cal.

She turns on him her look of mildly surprised interest. "What do you mean?"

"You were very quiet in the car and Mum didn't say anything about you being with us. I thought she was going to. I just wondered if there was any connection between the two."

"I was helping her to forget about me," Cal admits.

"I wish I could make her forget about me! How do you do it?"

"It was quite easy today because her mind was full of other things to think about. It was simple to put a little pressure on the part that was trying to remember to deal with me. She was helping in a way because she did not want to confront anyone today, she wanted to get away quickly."

"Could you do that with other people?" Victoria asks. "Then we wouldn't have any problem about what to do with you. You could just make people not notice you."

"I could only do it for a short time. When people are fully concentrating, it is hard to influence their minds," Cal replies regretfully.

"Well, I don't know what we are going to do with you after tomorrow," Brenton sighs. "I wish we could run away somewhere with you. If there really aren't any Narrangga left, maybe we could find another tribe, and go and live in the Outback with them where no one could find us."

Cal considers this for a moment. A gleam seems to come into her eyes, but then she shakes her head, smiling, as though reluctantly discarding an appealing idea. Victoria wonders suddenly what train of thought is going through her alien mind.

188 Cal points to the wall of the kiosk where bright orange and green letters proclaim DEADEN DEADEN DEADEN. "That's like on the store," she remarks. "What does it mean?"

Brenton shrugs. "The three slogans go together, in some way. You haven't seen the one on the hospital. I'll show it to you, if we go into Willstown. They're puns, like jokes. Dead End, Deaden, Dead N." He bites his lip as he remembers the significance of this last one as it occurred to him on the way to the cave, the night before.

"Is it some kind of custom?" Cal inquires. "Or does it have some sort of magical meaning?"

"Magical meaning? I wonder if it does. I hope it's not some sort of spell." Brenton laughs and shakes his head. "We don't really go in for that sort of thing. This is not a magical culture. It's more . . . someone feels they can't make any impression on things, or they haven't got any control over their life, so they go and paint on walls. It makes them feel important. And it's illegal, so they have to be brave and daring to do it."

He takes a bite out of his hamburger. "Yumm, this is fantastic. Don't you wish you could have a bite?"

"I would very much like to try the things you eat," Cal admits. "That would really be living the primitive life and getting back to nature. But the smell . . . !" She stops and shakes her head in awe.

"Does this smell bad?" Brenton asks, holding up the hamburger.

Cal makes an expressive face. "Terrible!"

"Oh!" Brenton eats it just the same. "Smells all right to me!"

"Your society must be weird if you don't have to feed yourselves," Victoria says. The conversation has started her thinking about how much time, effort and energy everybody puts into eating every day. She looks around now at the people gathered at the pool. Practically every one is either eating or drinking something. Even babies are crawling around holding onto their bottles! And all the signs and posters around the kiosk announce some kind of food, drink or smoke. "We do nothing but stuff things in our mouths!"

"It surprises me," Cal admits. "I had not realized other cultures spent so much time on eating and drinking."

"It is sort of revolting!" Victoria exclaims.

"No. A good anthropologist should never be revolted by an alien culture. Her job is to observe and record, not to judge."

"What else is different?" Brenton asks, finishing his hamburger and taking a rather self-conscious sip of orange juice. It is a large carton and he forgot to get a straw, so he has opened up the top to drink from it.

Cal makes a face that's a mixture of amusement and despair, like you make to a two-year-old who's just asked a question like How does television work. "Everything is different," she says. "It's nothing like here. I really can't explain it; there are too many things you simply do not have the terminology for. I suppose I could say it's a lot more organized and a lot more complex. There are very many things that we are not allowed to do. Our technology is very different and it is more far-reaching. Every aspect of life is controlled—that is why we have very few other life-forms, and what we have are all in special places, like zoos. We have no wild places, nothing like this." She gestures at the beach, the rocks and the sea beyond.

Brenton laughs. Farborough is hardly his idea of a wild place. Cal laughs too. "A lot of things seem really funny to me," she admits. "They have a sort of clumsiness that is almost charming. So ingenious and so unexpected. It is

190 nothing like the way we have evolved. Your culture is like a little backwater developing in such a strange way. I can understand why it comes to a dead end!"

Brenton shivers, despite the warmth of the sun on his bare back. He has the uncomfortable feeling he gets when he realizes he has made an error in a game and that his life is now over. There's never any warning; you just make a wrong decision at some stage, sometimes several moves before, and all of a sudden there's no way back. *Your part in this adventure is over. You have lost.* Cal's words reinforce a feeling he's had several times before, that at some stage in its existence his society took a fatal wrong turn, and that any moment now it will find itself unable to retrace its steps. It will be out of the game.

"It does come to a dead end, doesn't it?" he says quietly.

Cal looks away across the pool. She does not want to answer. Finally she says evasively, "All cultures do eventually."

"Will yours?"

"I don't know yet," she replies, and a new look, filling Victoria with deep unease, comes into her eyes as she stares at Brenton. "One of the reasons I came, apart from those I have mentioned to you already, was to see my own world from afar, to take a fresh look at it. It is hard to get a clear view of one's own society close up; you need to distance yourself from it to see where it is really heading. One of our problems is, our lives are very short. We do not turn into adults as you do."

"You mean there are only children in your world?"

"We do not have anything like your *parents*. This is a very interesting point. Presumably adults are only necessary if children need a long period of nurturing. Our growth to our standard size is very rapid, so our society is not split into adults and children."

"Excellent!" Brenton exclaims. "Take me there at once!" **191**

Victoria is once again filled with unease. She feels as though Cal is drawing Brenton in some way across to her side, leaving Victoria behind. "It must have its drawbacks too," she points out.

"We have to work very hard," Cal continues. "There is so much to pass on and so little time to do it in. We are very conscious of how little time each one of us has—only we do not call it time, of course. It is quite a different dimension, really. But that is why we never ask anyone how old she is. It would be like saying to her, You will be dead soon. Only," she amends her statement again, "we do not call it dead because the concept we have for what you call death is altogether different."

"Sometimes I get a flash of what you mean in my mind," Brenton says. "But when I try and put it into words it's impossible."

"The other problem we have," Cal goes on, "is that we are running out of seeds. One day we will have no new people growing and that will be the end of us. We will have reached our dead end. That is . . ." she adds.

"It's not what we call growing and they're not what we call seeds!" Brenton fills in with a laugh.

"Exactly!"

"Can't you get new ones from anywhere?" he asks.

Cal smiles again as though she has thought about the question and finds it fascinating. "I don't know."

Brenton is watching his sister on the opposite side of the pool. He thinks about her and Jason. He thinks about the goats, and the new male kids that will soon have to be killed and eaten. He thinks about the whole mysterious process of sex, and birth, and gender.

"What do you do for sex?" he asks.

"Tell me what you mean exactly by sex," Cal returns.

"It's the way we get new people," Brenton tries to explain

scientifically, but having embarked on the subject he finds it is making him uncomfortable. "But it's a whole lot more than that . . . it's when people love each other, and sometimes when they don't . . ."

"Go on," Vicky says, teasing him. "It's just the sort of thing anthropologists want to know about."

"You'd better explain it then," Brenton groans. "Doesn't your mother run a family planning clinic? You can be all technical about it."

Cal has taken the langscan out of her pocket and is checking *sex* out on it. She is quiet for a few moments as she concentrates on the silver card, then her face lightens and she says, "Ah!" with a new note in her voice.

"We have a similar sort of intimacy," she explains to Brenton and Victoria. "Only it is not physical. We reach it by linking minds. It is something very special to us, that we only do with equals who are also friends. If you undertake this mental intimacy together, you are committed to each other in a special way for as long as you live."

"Like being married," Victoria suggests.

"Can you do this, what you're talking about, with more than one person?" Brenton asks.

"Yes, you can do it with as many as you like but the commitment will always be there."

Brenton is fascinated. "Could you do it with one of us?"

Cal shakes her head. "It would not be right."

"Why not?"

She does not want to explain. She smiles and looks away. You would almost say she is embarrassed, Victoria thinks. She has a sudden insight why.

"She said among equals," she reminds Brenton.

"Does she think we're inferior?"

"We're very primitive to her."

Brenton finds this extremely funny. He's not ruffled or   **193** offended by the idea as Michael was. He's rather keen on this notion of mental intimacy; it sounds a lot easier to handle than physical intimacy, the hazards of which have been bothering him lately. He takes the dice out of his pocket and throws them casually on the concrete. He scoops them up and puts them back in his pocket. Cal watches him but says nothing.

"Do it with me," Brenton says, looking at her directly. Their eyes meet. Cal smiles as though she is tempted.

"Go on," Brenton urges. "It would be an interesting experiment. It might have great anthropological significance. Try it."

"It may not work with you."

"It probably won't," Brenton agrees. "So there's no harm in giving it a try."

"It's not safe," Cal goes on. "I don't know what it will do to you. The substances or methods any culture uses to produce ecstasy are very dangerous to those from another culture. This has always been true in all times and places. You may not be able to handle it, it may upset you in some way, it may be addictive. Anything may happen."

"She's right," Vicky puts in, alarmed. "It's better not to mess around with it."

"Like white man's firewater," Brenton says scornfully. "Just give me a little dose then!"

The way Cal is studying Brenton is frightening Victoria more and more. She has got into the habit of seeing the dark-skinned girl as a child, more or less the same age as herself. She keeps forgetting that in real terms Cal is an adult being, a scientist of advanced intelligence and culture. Now it comes back to her with a disturbing jolt. Cal is assessing Brenton with a scientist's eye, calculating and impersonal. Smiling a slow, secret smile she says, "Very well."

Brenton swallows hard. His mouth is suddenly dry. "What do I do?" he asks.

"Don't do anything. Just keep your mind open and quiet."

He looks nervously around the pool at the shouting children, noticing among them Michael, with Danny and Craig. "We're just going to do it here? With everyone looking?"

"They won't notice anything. It all happens only in the mind."

"Brenton," Victoria pleads. "Don't do it. Come on, let's go and swim, or get an ice cream or something!" She half stands; Brenton does not move.

"You go if you want to. I'll come when it's over. How long does it take, Cal?"

"It seems like a long time," she explains. "But in reality it takes no more than a second."

16

THE THREE are sitting on the concrete terrace above the pool. Behind them the sky is a clear, bright summer blue. In front of them the sea is beginning to fill the pool. The waves ebb and flow ceaselessly, the splash of the water merging with the shrieks of children. Seagulls, white against the blue sky, add their mewing to the pattern of sound.

Brenton and Cal look at each other. Their eyelids close.

Brenton can still hear the children, the waves and the seagulls. He can still feel the warmth of the sun on his skin, but the ordinary, everyday world has faded into the background and something else is taking its place. Other scenes are being superimposed over it. They move so quickly he hardly has time to realize what they are, and they produce in him a succession of rapid and intense emotions, stronger than anything he has ever felt in his life before, seductive and irresistible.

It is like actually living a fantasy adventure, full of heroism, terror, suspense and excitement, more gripping and poignant than he would have dreamed possible. And the person he is living it with is Cal. They become friend and enemy to each other, brother, sister, destroyer, savior, ally and lover, as they explore all possible relationships in all their intensity and their power. It fills him with wonder and fear, awe and joy and exultation, and finally all these blend in a tremendous love for the being at his side.

He wants it to go on forever, but the love is darkened suddenly by a sensation that frightens him in a completely new way. It is as though all the fears that have dogged his life lately have taken over Cal's body and face and now they are confronting him. For a moment he is terrified of her, and then the feeling changes slightly, and his terror is not of her but for her. He feels her mind tremble and falter, as his own is doing. He knows there is something wrong with her, he has felt it in his own bones, a creeping sickness that she is about to lose the battle against. He knows she is afraid of dying, and he knows he has to try to take her home.

They open their eyes and stare at each other in horror. Cal's usually adult eyes are made vulnerable by fear.

The noise of the swimming pool increases until Brenton can pick out words among the hubbub, and across the pool he clearly hears his brother's voice saying cheerfully to a friend, "Get stuffed!" Then, closer, he hears someone saying, "Dirty black!"

196 He glances away and sees the world around him with a new and painful vision. He looks back helplessly at Cal, but she is no longer looking at him. Her head is bowed and she is staring at her foot. It is swollen and red, and streaks of purple run from it up her leg.

"What happened?" Vicky is saying, looking anxiously from one to the other. "Did anything happen? What was it like?" And then, urgently, she demands, "Brenton, are you all right?"

On the terrace below them a group of boys is watching them with idle curiosity. Brenton recognizes them from school; one of them is Wayne Smith. They are smoking, and drinking cans of beer and Coke. From where Brenton is sitting they look like huge, blond giants. He is aware of being small and dark, and that Cal and Vicky are small and dark too, and that they will never, any of them, be anything but outsiders here.

One of the blond giants calls up lazily, "Hey, Trethewan, are you off with the fairies again? And who's your cotton-picking friend?"

He doesn't have to throw the dice to choose how to act. He does it quite instinctively. It's as though something red and black bursts inside his head. In one swift movement he leaps to his feet and throws the orange juice he is still holding directly into Wayne's face.

The giants are too astonished to move. Before they have time to stop saying "You little bastard," get to their feet and grab him, Brenton has run on up the steps, out of the pool area and down the road. His breath is coming in sobs, and tears are scalding his eyes. He hates the world he lives in; he hates it and he is ashamed of it. He runs as though he could run away from it and leave it far behind.

17 BUT HE cannot run away from his family. Five minutes later the Falcon draws up alongside him. He is walking down the road, wiping his eyes on his hand, still sobbing and swearing to himself, not knowing if he is more angry than sad, or more sad than angry. He has a frantic feeling he must get out, but he doesn't know what he's escaping from or where he's running to.

"Get in the car," Shelley shouts at him. He gets in, but only because Cal is on the backseat next to Vicky. When they're moving again she says furiously, looking at him in the rearview mirror, "Whatever happened to you, Brenton? You promised Mum you'd be sensible. Whatever came over you? Wayne says he'll go to the police! He'll have us barred from the pool!"

"You went berserk!" Michael says. "Gee it was funny! I've never seen anything like Wayne's face. Orange juice all over it, and his nose bleeding where the edge of the carton caught it. You've got it coming to you, you know, Brenton. He swore he'd get you. He'll murder you. Trust you to pick the only Kung Fu expert in Penbowie!"

"But why?" Shelley demands angrily. "Everyone was just having a quiet sunbake at the pool. You weren't even talking to Wayne. And suddenly out of the blue you throw orange juice all over him. Why?"

Brenton doesn't answer. On reflection it does not seem the wisest thing to have done and no doubt Wayne is even now dreaming up some vicious plan of revenge which will catch up with him sooner or later, next term if not before. But he cannot explain to Shelley the absolute compulsion that made him defend Cal. She is sitting next to him, looking at him gravely as though assessing him. He is aware of the presence of her mind just on the boundary of his, and he is aware too that at any time their two minds can merge again in that profound and shattering way. He gives a sigh and smiles at her.

"I don't see what you've got to laugh about!" Shelley says, turning the wheel sharply to enter the driveway.

"I'm afraid it was my fault," Cal says, but the way she says it irritates Shelley even further.

"Yes, I thought you might have had something to do with it," she snaps, braking to negotiate the bend. She doesn't say anything until they stop outside the house, and then she lets out her breath in a sigh and turns to look at Cal.

"I think you'd better push off to wherever it is you've come from. You're causing a lot of trouble and I don't want you hanging around here while my parents are away."

There's a moment of silence while Cal's eyes flick from Brenton to Vicky and back again.

Shelley's basic good nature gets the better of her. "I mean, I don't want to be rude but . . ."

"She can't go, Shell," Brenton says quietly. "She's not going yet. She hasn't got anywhere to go. Not yet, anyway," he adds, after another quick look at Cal.

Victoria feels her neck prickle as though all the tiny hairs along the back of it are standing on end. Something has happened and she has missed exactly what it was, but it has given her a strong feeling of apprehension. She shivers. "You shouldn't have done it!" she accuses Cal, her unease deepening into hostility.

"Shouldn't have done what?" Shelley asks as she gets out of the car and shuts the door with a slam. But then the two cats approach her to say hello, and, as she bends down to tickle one of them under the chin, both Brenton and Cal gaze at her silently. The other cat weaves between her legs and disappears under the car. Shelley straightens up and looks around at the countryside, stretching away to the sea. The weather is changing. The sky is becoming opaque, and it is still and oppressive.

"What are we going to do now?" Shelley says. She has forgotten what she was saying about Cal.

"Danny's mum said I could stay the night," Mick says. "I think I'll get my things and go on over there. Will you take me?" he adds hopefully.

"What, just to Penbowie?"

"I've got to take my sleeping bag."

"Okay, then, and I might go and see Joanne for a little while. Can you stay out of trouble till I get back?" This last remark is directed fiercely to Brenton, who is going toward the house with Vicky and Cal, but he pretends not to hear it.

18 MICHAEL tears out of the house with his sleeping bag and his fishing gear and jumps into the front seat of the car. Shelley gets in and carefully puts it into reverse. As it begins to move backward there's a brown flash from under the front wheel, and a cat dashes away across the yard.

"Cripes," Shelley gasps in horror. "I nearly ran over Tang."

19 "YOU SHOULDN'T have done it!" Vicky repeats to Cal. They are now in Brenton's room and Cal is sitting on the bed, her feet raised in front of her, her head drooping. Without looking at Victoria she replies, "No, maybe not. However it is done now, we cannot go back and undo it." Her voice has not lost its precise, scientific tone, but it has something new added to it that Vicky has not heard before, something that makes her sound more like a child.

"What's the matter with her?" She puts the question to Brenton; she is too angry with Cal to speak to her directly.

"Look at her foot," Brenton replies. "Didn't you notice she could hardly walk from the car?"

Cal's foot is swollen to twice the size it should be and beneath the dark skin are streaks of purple. Victoria puts her hand out and touches it very, very gently. It is hot and tight and shiny. Cal winces and gives a cry, not exactly of pain, more of amazement.

"It's bad," Victoria says to Brenton. "She should have it looked at."

"Who by?" he replies. "We can't take her to a doctor. People will ask too many questions. And she doesn't want us to."

"What does she want?"

"She wants to go back," Brenton answers for her. "She wants me to take her to the cave tonight, and they'll come and get her."

"Who'll come and get her?"

"Oh, Vicky," he bursts out in exasperation. "I can't explain it to you . . . I don't even know myself if it's who, or what—we just don't have the words for it. All I know is, I've got to get her there and it's me that . . ."

He stops abruptly as if he has decided not to tell her the rest. Victoria stares at him and then to her astonishment she receives a perfectly clear image of Brenton and Cal together in a place that she does not recognize in any sense at all. "She wants to take you with her, doesn't she?"

Brenton looks directly at Victoria and nods.

Cal looks at her too, with approval. "You read his mind just then," she informs her with great satisfaction. "That is very interesting. And the rhythms between you are very interesting right now, too. How I wish I could stay longer. But I'm afraid I will be seriously ill if I do not get back to civilization."

"Yes, I can understand that you've got to go," Victoria replies. "But you can't take Brenton with you. He belongs here; this is his world. He can't just disappear."

"He will be quite safe with me," Cal assures her. "There is so much he can tell me about this extraordinary civilization of yours. If I ever come back he can act as my interpreter. And he will be living proof to my colleagues that your culture really exists."

There is a gleam of professional enthusiasm in her eyes that Victoria finds repelling. "He's not some sort of specimen," she exclaims hotly. "He's a human being. And what about his family? Imagine how they'll miss him!"

"They do not appear to be very fond of him," Cal observes in surprise.

"That doesn't mean they don't love him," she retorts. "Brenton," she appeals to him. "You're not serious, are

202 you?"

"I don't know," he replies, his eyes turned away from her.

"It's something to do with that thing you did together at the pool, that mind thing, isn't it?"

"I've got to do it again," he admits. "It was just fantastic. I can't describe it to you." Just thinking about it makes his face light up and his eyes shine.

Victoria looks at him helplessly. "You should never have tried it," she groans. "I told you not to." Then a new thought occurs to her. "She knew that would happen!" she cries. "Cal knew it would happen. She planned it. She always wanted to take someone back with her. She was hunting you, and now she's trapped you."

"I don't know if she planned it," he replies seriously. "But once it all started to happen, she may have taken advantage of it, I can see that. But now I have to help her. I have to defend and look after her. That's why I chucked the orange juice at Wayne at the pool. He was starting to hassle her and I just couldn't help myself. It probably wasn't such a good idea," he admits after a moment. "But I had to stand up for Cal in some way and that was the first thing that occurred to me."

"Victim of the old brain," Cal interrupts from the bed with the ghost of a smile.

"It's a way out," Brenton goes on, looking straight at Victoria now. "I thought I was stuck in a dead end, and suddenly there's a way out. I'm going to be rescued. Rescued from all this," he gestures around the room at the nuclear weapons. "Rescued from Wayne Smith, who's going to pulverize me next time he sees me. Rescued from being schizophrenic, like Mum thinks, or something like that. Rescued from having to grow up to be someone like Dad . . ."

203

"Don't be silly," she cries. "You can't just opt out of it all!"

"Why not?" He gives her a challenging look, and takes the dice out of his pocket. He begins to throw them from hand to hand.

"You're not going to throw the dice to decide!" Victoria cries, trying to grab them out of his hand. They fall to the floor.

"Too late," Brenton says. "They're already thrown." They lie there; double six uppermost. "That settles it then," he murmurs.

He picks the dice up and gives Victoria a grin. It's full of bravado, but underneath she senses uncertainty and fear. She cries out to them: "How do you know things will be any better where Cal comes from? They'll probably be just as bad, if not worse. It doesn't sound like a very nice place. And Cal may not be alive for long there, for all you know. She might be just about to die from old age."

"Shh," Brenton interrupts her. "Don't talk so loud, she might hear you."

"I want her to hear me," Vicky protests, speaking louder still. "I want her to think twice about what she's going to do to you. She can't just come here and steal boys away!" Something else occurs to her and she stops in full flight, her eyes horrified.

"It's boys you want, isn't it?" she accuses Cal. "Because you only have one sex, and you're running out of seeds . . . is that the real reason you came here?"

"No." Cal denies it, shaking her head wearily.

Vicky stares at her for a few seconds, biting her lip, wondering if she will ever know the truth. Then she returns to the attack on Brenton. "You can't just run away
204 from everything, Brenton. You've got to stay and help sort

the world out. Nothing's going to be solved by running away."

"There's nothing I can do," he points out. "Mum's right, there's nothing any one person can do; it's all too difficult."

"Yeah, so you take the easy way out and run!" A note of scorn comes into her voice. "I thought you cared more than that. But you just want to save yourself—the rest of the world can go to hell."

"It deserves to go to hell," he replies, starting to shout now. "Look at it, look at all the people in it! It's had it. It was a nice experiment, but it failed. It's all totally and completely screwed up."

"How can you say that!" Vicky gestures forcefully at the garden outside, shimmering and beautiful in the afternoon sun. "You must be blind! This place is lovely. Your family is great." She stares at his cold, closed, unconvinced face and stamps her foot in exasperation. "Honestly, Brenton, I could shake you! You don't know you're born."

She turns and runs swiftly out of the room. Brenton sinks down on the bed next to Cal, his face in his hands. When Vicky comes back she's holding the wall hanging Chris made for her. "Look at this," she says fiercely. "Look at it. It's wonderful; it's a work of art." She holds it up so he can see the blue and gold colors that echo the garden and the sea. "Don't you see, it's worth doing something like this. It's adding something to the world. It counts for something. You do what you can, where you can, and it all adds up."

"And that's going to change the world," he says scornfully, getting off the bed and crossing the room to the window.

"If you're going to change the world you've got to start somewhere."

When he speaks again, his back is to the light, so she

cannot see his face, "I can't start making wall hangings," he says. "Everyone thinks I'm peculiar enough already without that!"

"I didn't think you cared what other people think!"

"No, I don't," he returns seriously. "What I'm saying is that you may be able to content yourself with things like gardens, and wall hangings, and all those beautiful things. But I can't. Perhaps it's easier for girls," he adds as an afterthought.

"Perhaps what's easier?" she demands, suspecting him of patronizing her.

"Growing up, knowing who you're meant to be, enjoying life, the whole process. Do you know what I think? I don't think the future belongs to men anymore—not to Western men. They've screwed it all up too much. It's someone else's turn to have a shot at it—women, other races, other cultures. People like her." Brenton points at Cal. "That's why I'd rather go with her than stay here."

"What about your parents? They'll be devastated."

"They won't! They'll probably give a huge sigh of relief. They won't have to worry about whether I'm normal or not anymore. Besides," he adds unfairly, "they've got you now. I'm sure you'll make a much more satisfactory child than I've ever been."

"What about me?" Victoria demands, playing her last card without much hope. "I'll miss you terribly."

Despite himself, Brenton is moved by this appeal. He attempts to hide it. "Get away, Vicky. You don't care one way or the other!"

"I do! I like you more than anyone else I know!"

He grins at her, embarrassed but pleased. "Well, why don't you come too?"

Victoria stands frowning at him, silent for a full minute.

She is thinking she would not have to go to boarding school, she would not have to get used to living at the Trethewans', she too could escape from a way of life that she has discovered she does not really like anymore.

"Don't be silly," she says finally. "You know I can't."

20

THERE IS a pause that seems to last forever. The afternoon breeze from the sea suddenly awakes and sets tinkling the wind chimes that hang outside on the veranda. A blowfly buzzes erratically against the screen and then is quiet. The two children feel as though they are standing at an axis, a point of perfect balance between what is and what might be, the meeting point of two different worlds. Neither of them dares move or speak.

The one who speaks into this poised silence is Cal.

"Throw the dice!" Her eyes are bright and feverish, her voice harsh and urgent. She is not speaking to Brenton or to Victoria. She is speaking to *you*. You who have been the observer so far. You who have been watching the whole story.

Throw the dice!

CHOICES

IV

If you threw over 6

1 THE SILENCE is broken and the world starts up again. Brenton is staring at Victoria, but before either of them can say anything, there's the sound of a car coming up the drive, cut short suddenly by the squeal of brakes and a horrible, terminating thump.

"What the hell was that?"

Brenton runs through the kitchen, opens the screen door, and sees something he has always feared to see: a small brown body lying under the wheel of Jason's Valiant, angled out in the improbable but unmistakable attitude of death. Jason is standing white-faced and horrified by the car, explaining, "I didn't see him! Geez, I'm sorry. He ran right out in front of the car. I didn't see him at all. I felt the bump and I tried to brake but it was too late. Poor little fellow. Still, it would have been instantaneous. He wouldn't have felt a thing."

"Shut up!" Brenton yells at him. He is kneeling by the dead cat, stroking him gently. The soft fur is dusty. "Tang," he murmurs, "Tang," and carefully brushes the dust away. Blood is coming from the animal's nose and mouth, dark, congealing fast, dirty with gravel. Brenton picks him up, his face stark and unbelieving. Now he has blood all over his shirt. "No," he whispers. "No."

He feels as though he is holding in his hands a whole era of his life, dead and lost forever. A hundred memories **211** flood through him: Tang on his shoulders, Tang asking to be fed, Tang yowling in welcome when the family came home, Tang the familiar spirit of the place, idiosyncratic and faithful, Tang, his totem. His chest heaves as a sob forces its way out.

There's another squeal of brakes as Shelley pulls up in the Falcon. "Did you get the fish-and-chips, Jason?" she calls out cheerfully, but the smile is wiped from her face as she takes in the scene.

"Oh Brenton," she says helplessly. "Oh Brenton, how awful!" She puts her arm around his shoulders and tries to hug him, but he is rigid and unresponsive.

"Geez, I'm sorry," Jason says again.

"It wasn't your fault," Shelley says in a small unhappy voice, close to tears too. "I nearly did the same thing this afternoon."

2 CAL'S BLACK eyes jerk open as Brenton comes into the room where she is lying crumpled on the bed. He has just buried his cat in the garden and his hands are covered with blood.

"What happened?" she whispers.

"Tang was killed," he replies after a moment, turning toward her with a look of hopelessness.

Her face takes on an expression of grief identical to his own. "I'm sorry," she says softly. "He was a beautiful life-form. And very intelligent."

"Yeah," Brenton agrees with a sigh, sitting down on the 212 bed next to her. "He was the greatest. One of a kind."

She starts to scrabble around weakly but urgently on the bed. Then she sits up, her face contorted with anxiety.

"Brenton, where's the langscan? I've forgotten where I put it."

"It must be in your pocket. You had it at the pool."

Cal pushes herself painfully up into a sitting position and feels in the pocket of the shorts that used to be Brenton's.

"I recorded the cat on the langscan," she says, taking it out with feeble fingers. "You can hear the playback, if you like."

He frowns at her, not understanding.

"Look into it," she tells him, and Brenton does so, curiously. He feels it connect with his brain, the same way the silver disk of the braingame does. Then he feels within him a sort of furry, clever, feline essence that he recognizes instantly as Tang. His grief-stricken face softens in amazement and delight.

3 VICTORIA is sitting on her bed. Through the open door she can see Brenton coming out of the bathroom. He has just washed his hands clean of earth and blood. His eyes are still red from crying, but his face is calm and composed as though he has come to a decision. She calls to him in alarm.

"Brenton!"

He stands in the doorway and looks across the room at her. The space between them seems as vast as that between her and Cal when they first met, a long, long time ago. He is already a universe away.

"You're going, aren't you?"

He looks at her as though she is speaking a foreign language. When he has decoded it he replies, "I've got to."

"Brenton," Shelley calls down the passageway. "Come and try and eat something."

"I'm not hungry," he shouts back, opens his mouth to say something to Victoria, closes it again, shrugs his shoulders and disappears into his room, shutting the door firmly behind him.

Shelley calls again, "You want some fish-and-chips, Vicky?"

4 BRENTON stares out of the window at the coast and the sea beyond, waiting impatiently for night. One by one stars are appearing in the darkening sky. Behind him on Michael's bed, Cal tosses and mutters. Her eyes are closed and her hair lies damply on her neck and forehead. Brenton is receiving from her delirious nightmares that he cannot understand and that fill him with terror. He knows he must get her to the cave and then transmit with all his strength, since she is no longer able to send any message to whomever is waiting for her call.

He is waiting for Jason to go home too, but the Valiant remains obstinately stationary outside the back of the house. Opening the door of his bedroom he listens intently. There is no longer any sound from the family room or the kitchen. He creeps down the passageway: the house seems deserted.

Then from Shelley's room he hears a stifled giggle and

whispering. He tiptoes to the door and listens. The whispering gives way to other noises, hurried, yielding and intimate, that make his face go hot in the darkness. That murderer! he thinks irrationally. How could she?

However, it sounds as though they will be occupied for some time to come. He returns to his room and shakes Cal gently. She opens her eyes abruptly and stares at him as though she has no idea who he is. She mutters something in her own language and tosses her head from side to side.

"Cal!" he calls softly but commandingly. She focuses her gaze on him, and he holds it with his own. "I'm taking you to the cave soon," he says. "Do you think you can stand up?"

"Help me!" her mind says clearly to his.

"I am helping you," his returns, but she cannot receive him.

"Help me!" her mind transmits again.

Brenton frowns and sighs. He tries again, more urgently this time, "Cal! Cal! Stand up!" He puts his arms around her and pulls her up on the bed. She seems to understand what he is doing; she slides her legs over and puts her feet to the ground, but when he pulls her up and her weight presses on the infected foot, she gives another cry of astonishment and crumples back down onto the bed. Sweat trickles from her forehead, and she retches.

"Oh God!" Brenton doesn't know if he's swearing or praying. He lays her back on the bed and goes to get Vicky.

5 VICTORIA has gone from crying to sleeping to dreaming. In her dream a small brown cat has fallen into the water and is trying to clamber back into the dinghy, but Wayne Smith is clubbing it on the head and shouting, "All the beautiful life-forms must be destroyed!"

"Vicky!"

The cat has turned into Brenton and Wayne is hitting him viciously over the head.

"Vicky!"

She wakes up and Brenton is there in the room with her. He puts his mouth close to her ear and hisses, "Cal has got much worse. I've got to get her away, but she can't walk. You'll have to help me carry her."

This seems less real than her dream was. She blinks at him.

"Get up, Vicky!" he orders her. "You've got to help me get Cal to the caves."

6 HALF-AWAKE as she is Victoria can see that Cal is desperately ill. She looks thinner than ever, as if she is fading away, and there is a defeated look about her that strikes Victoria at the heart. She puts aside her previous unease and distrust. Now all she wants is to get Cal to the place where she can be rescued as quickly as possible.

"What about getting her own clothes?" she whispers to Brenton. But when he goes softly out to the shed and brings back the pack, the strange material will not open for them.

"Still, we'll have to take it with us," Brenton mutters. "Good thing you thought of it. We must get going. I'll take her under the shoulders, you carry her legs. But don't touch her foot whatever you do."

It's much harder than it sounds. By the time they have got the half-conscious figure to the back door their muscles are aching, and the effort of doing it, and doing it quietly, has made them nearly frantic. Victoria can feel fear building up inside her and threatening to take her over; fear of being discovered, fear of Cal dying, fear of Brenton leaving. The death of the cat, on top of all the emotional upheaval of the last few weeks, has left her tearful and jumpy. She feels far too fragile to cope with any more.

"We can't carry her all the way through the town," she whispers. "And if we can't run we'll never get past the dog at the shack."

They both see the Valiant at the same time. In the manner of all stationary cars, it is standing there waiting to be used.

"Could you drive it, Brenton?"

"I've driven it heaps of times before, in the yard and up and down the drive."

"What about the keys?"

They are still inside, left there when Jason leaped from the car after it killed Tang.

"Vicky, open the back door. I'll put Cal on the backseat and you sit next to her and hang on to her." Between them they manage to get Cal inside, but they can't do it very gently, and she cries out again.

"Sorry!" Brenton groans, biting his lip as though he feels the pain himself. Then he gets in the front, shuts the door quietly and starts to fiddle with the switches.

"What are you doing?" Victoria whispers.

"I can't find the lights. I've never driven at night." Suddenly there's a click, and a flash of light illuminates the yard. Brenton extinguishes it swiftly. "Too bright," he mutters. "I'll put them on when we get to the road." He takes a deep breath and turns on the ignition.

The engine sounds as loud as a jet plane in the still night. The car leaps forward.

"Damn!" Brenton swears, banging his head on the steering wheel and biting his tongue. "I forgot to check if it was in neutral."

"Take the handbrake off," Victoria hisses, as the car bumps and jerks across the yard. "And get into second quickly!"

He is having difficulty reaching the pedals, and as he lets the clutch up the engine stalls. He swears again; the car is now on the sloping driveway and is rolling gently downhill.

"Put it in first," Victoria suggests from the backseat, "and jump it out; the engine'll start again."

"OK, OK," he grunts, doing just that. "You don't have to be a backseat driver, Vick. I do know what I'm doing." He's got it under control now; it was just the first few terrifying moments of handling the car on his own that threw him. Now they are progressing in third gear fairly smoothly down the driveway toward the road. Brenton puts on the lights and the wipers, turns off the wipers and finds the turn signals instead. Then he remembers to step on the brake, and manages to do it without stalling the engine. The Valiant shudders to a halt, its nose peering out at the edge of 218 the road.

The headlights light up the new galvanized iron fence that runs along the front of the shack. And picked out in glowing shades of orange and green, gleaming in the incandescence of the lights, are the words DEAD END DEAD END DEAD END.

"Wow!" Brenton breathes, staring at it for several seconds, as the engine ticks noisily over. "He must have only just finished it. We must have just missed him. That'll fix them," he adds with some satisfaction. "Serves them right!" He peers out into the roadway. "Anything coming? No. Here goes then," and he turns the wheel carefully, taking his foot off the brake. The car responds, inching its way out. Into second, a little more speed, and into third. He decides that's fast enough for the time being.

"Something's coming toward us," Vicky says as headlights rake the sky ahead. Brenton slows right down.

"Change down," Vicky reminds him, as a truck hurtles past them, its frame lit up with white and orange lights.

"Wow!" Brenton exclaims again. "That's scary! It feels like it's coming right at you."

"Go a bit faster," Vicky says. "Suppose Jason's heard us and he's following us?"

Brenton looks in the rearview mirror and realizes he can't see a thing in it. He should have checked it before they left, but he forgot. "Take a look out the back, Vicky," he says, stepping on the accelerator a little. "Tell me if there's anything coming."

7 THEY HAVE nearly reached Penbowie when another vehicle approaches them. Brenton swears at its driver when its lights remain high, dazzling him, and then he swears again, when he recognizes the 4WD from the shack. And he's sure that a face is staring down at him from the front seat in amazed recognition, as the vehicle races past.

"Vicky," he says. "I think they might have recognized us. And they'll see the graffiti when they get to the shack. They're sure to think we did it! They'll probably turn around and come right back after us!"

He is struck again by the same sense of inevitability, of the curious destiny that is linking all the separate strands of his life as though he himself willed that the phantom graffiti artist should write on that particular fence at that precise moment, as though he is playing out a fantasy game in which all the rules have been written and the moves preordained—a game which is now approaching its climax and its end. He steps on the accelerator again and the Valiant speeds up.

8 IT'S SPEEDING up a little too much when they come through the car park up to the seawall, and Brenton doesn't brake quite soon enough, not realizing it takes so long for a car to come to a halt.

"Brake!" Vicky yells from the backseat, but the car stops anyway with a hefty jolt and a crumpling noise of metal, followed by a little tinkling of glass. Cal moans. "Help me!" Brenton hears in his head.

"How's she doing?" he asks Vicky.

"She's hot, she's burning." Vicky lays her hand gently on the dark forehead. "Brenton, is she going to die?"

"Not if I can get her back home again," he replies, and home no longer means his home, but hers.

He opens the car door and climbs out. He is shaking from the tension of the drive. He glances briefly at the damage to the front of the car. "Jason's going to kill me!" he mutters to himself. Jason, Pam, his parents, Wayne Smith, not to mention the nuclear forces of the superpowers—they are all after him, the whole pack of them, streaming after him like dogs after a rabbit, but he's going to get away from them. They think they have him boxed up in a dead end, but he's going to escape them. The thought fills him with mad elation. He runs to the back of the car and swings open the door.

"Come on, Vicky," he says urgently. "Let's hurry."

Michael and Danny, not sleeping but talking in Danny's room, hear the thump as the Valiant hits the wall, quite clearly.

"What on earth was that?" Michael demands.

"Someone's had a few too many! Let's go and have a look."

9 THE WIND has swung around and is blowing up strongly from the southwest, and from the same direction a huge mass of cloud is approaching, swallowing up the stars one by one. The sea is whipping up into choppy waves. The temperature has dropped, and Brenton and Victoria shiver as they regard the expanse of rocky beach they have to cross with the half-conscious Cal.

"I think I'd better try and carry her on my own," Brenton decides. "I'll take her over my shoulder in a fireman's lift. You walk next to me and help to steady her and hold the flashlight so we can see a little."

Cal says, in a moment of lucidity as he lifts her, "I am sorry to be so much trouble to you," and he receives from her a feeling of embarrassment at being so weak and dependent on savages like themselves that at another time would have made him laugh.

"Have you got the pack, Vicky?" Brenton staggers as he turns to go down the steps, but Vicky has her hand under his arm, and she holds him up. Cal is not heavy—she is as light and insubstantial as a fern—but they cannot go as fast as he would like. Despite the flashlight it is too dark to see much and the wind is whistling around their legs and ankles. They both slip and stumble over unseen rocks, and several times Brenton nearly falls.

222

10 "THAT'S Jason's car," Michael says in surprise as he and Danny survey its damaged radiator and headlights. "What on earth do you think he was doing?"

"Kissing your sister, probably!" Danny stares out over the beach. "Where do you think they are now?"

Peering down the beach they can see the erratic gleam of the flashlight.

"Funny place to take your girlfriend," Danny remarks.

"Let's go and spy on them!" Michael suggests.

11 FINALLY Brenton stops and whispers to Vicky, "I think we must be nearly there."

He turns toward the land and takes a few tentative steps in the direction of the cliff face. "We're at the caves, Vicky. Which one was she in when you first met her?"

"The biggest one, that faces up toward the shack," Vicky replies. Even though it's almost pitch-dark she remembers her way around the cave area perfectly, by feel, as though the memories have been locked up in the cells of her body just waiting for this moment. Holding Brenton by the arm she guides him to the cave entrance.

Once inside, out of the wind, he lifts Cal off his back and settles down on the ground with her leaning up against him.

"Cal," he hisses in her ear. "Cal, can you talk to me? You have to tell me what to do." He can feel her mind stir reluctantly as he tries to reach it. She opens her eyes and stares at him. "Tell me what to do," he begs again.

"Need my pack," she breathes painfully back.

"Give me the pack, Vicky. And hold the flashlight so we can see what we're doing."

"How are we going to open it?" Vicky asks as she hands it to him.

"You'll have to open it for me," he tells Cal. There are a few moments of silence while her eyelids flicker open and shut over the feverish black eyes, and then she extends her hand weakly. Brenton puts the pack into it. Her fingers claw at it and it opens a fraction. She plucks at it again and manages to get her hand inside. She pulls something out, but shakes her head at it. It is a small disk, one of the braingames. Vicky takes it from her.

"Yes," Cal whispers. "That one for you . . . need something else . . ."

She reaches back into the pack and manages to extract another disk, rather larger. She fixes her dark eyes on Brenton and nods. "Transmitter . . ."

He puts his hand out and holds it, looking at her questioningly.

"You have to do it with your mind," Cal whispers. "It will respond to you, just like the braingame. You can do it, Brenton. I will help you as much as I can. They are waiting to hear from me. They will send a transport wave and it will take me and anything else that is here with me. Do you understand, Brenton?"

"Yes, I understand," he replies, almost impatiently. "I've got to come with you. You are too weak to do the transmitting on your own, and the transport wave can't differentiate and take you but leave me. I understand that. . . .

It's all right," he continues when she tries to speak again. "I want to come. I'm choosing to do it."

The reality of what he is saying hits Victoria like a blow. "No, Brenton!" she pleads.

"Vicky," Cal breathes again. "Vicky must go away . . . may get taken too, may be violent . . ."

"Yeah, good point," Brenton says. His voice is quite calm, but Victoria wishes she could see his face. "Better go, Vicky. Get right away from the cave."

The tears that threatened her before now rise into her eyes. "Don't do it, Brenton," she sobs. She is kneeling on the damp cave floor beside him. She reaches out now and clings around his neck. He turns his head, feels the tears on her cheeks and kisses her lips awkwardly.

"Don't worry," he whispers to her. "I'll get back again sometime. I promise you. Now go on, get outside."

"Good-bye, Vicky," Cal whispers so faintly Victoria hardly hears it.

12

TEARS ARE dropping on her hands as she crawls out backward. The wind has risen to a gale, and like tears huge drops of rain are beginning to fall. Down on the beach, on the seawall, she can see the glimmer of headlights, and she thinks she hears the sound of a car door slamming, and voices, before the wind whips them away. A few meters from the entrance to the cave she turns and stands there, waiting. One hand holds the brain-game Cal has given her. The other is feeling the beads of the necklace at her throat.

There's a tiny glimmer in front of her, as though some- **225** thing is peeling back, and then the darkness itself seems to split open momentarily. She is blinded by the sudden dazzling light, but in her mind she has a clear picture of Cal and Brenton, one moment in the cave, the next *somewhere else*, though still visible to her, still together.

Then the light and the picture vanish as the roof of the cave collapses inward and the full weight of the cliff crashes down onto the rocky floor.

13 THE NEXT THING Victoria is aware of is something wet and scratchy under her cheek, and she can't think what it is, because surely she is in bed and has been dreaming. She moves her head a little to try and get away from it, then she is conscious of a bright light on the other side of her eyelids. She thinks she won't open her eyes yet; she's not even sure if she can, but she knows it will hurt if she tries.

"She's alive! Oh, thank God, she's alive!"

Victoria knows that voice but she's never heard it like this before, full of tears and almost gentle.

"Don't move, honey," the voice reassures her. "You're going to be all right. We're here now. You're going to be all right."

There are men's voices, shocked and filled with grief and astonishment, more bright lights, exclamations of disbelief and horror, and then she opens her eyes, because Michael is kneeling beside her, and his voice is saying over and over again, "Where's Brenton? Vicky, where's Brenton?"

226   "It's OK," she whispers, trying to make out his face in

the harsh light. "They got away before it caved in. Brenton and Cal got away."

"Where are they?" he insists, his voice starting to choke with anguish.

"They got away," she repeats. She turns her head with a huge effort and looks at the other person kneeling beside her. It is Pam, and she is shaking her head, and tears are starting to pour down her cheeks.

14

THE BODIES are never found, but everyone assumes Brenton Trethewan and an unknown girl died in the landslide on the night of the big storm. A memorial service is held for them, and Brenton has twelve separate notices in the Deaths column of the local paper, including one from Wayne Smith and his family.

Victoria goes to boarding school at the end of the holidays, taking the necklace and the braingame with her, along with the wall hanging. She isn't allowed to wear the necklace at school of course, but she wears it at night while she practices with the braingame. One night, she knows it, one night she will reach them. One night she will talk to Brenton and Cal again.

If you threw 6 or under

1 THE SILENCE is broken and the world starts up again. Brenton is staring at Victoria, but before either of them can say anything there is the sound of a car coming up the drive, followed by the squeal of brakes. A few seconds later they hear the Falcon arrive too. The car doors slam, the screen door slams and Shelley calls out to them, "Jason's brought some fish-and-chips, kids. Come and eat!"

Brenton looks from Vicky to Cal and back again. "What are we going to do?"

"I don't know," she replies rather desperately. Whenever she's been feeling desperate lately she's got into the habit of feeling the beads of the necklace, which she's been wearing constantly. She does this now, and it gives her an idea. "Do you think this would help her?" she asks, taking it off, her neck feeling suddenly empty and light.

"Try it," Brenton replies. Victoria lifts the hot fragile head and slips the necklace over it. Cal smiles a little, her eyes close and her breathing deepens.

"Leave her to sleep for a bit," Vicky suggests. "Let's eat and see how she is afterward."

"OK," he agrees. The smell of fish-and-chips is penetrating the house, tantalizing.

Jason is sitting back to front on a chair at the kitchen
table. "That cat of yours just used up another of his nine

lives," he remarks with a relieved laugh. "I swear he went right under the car."

"I nearly hit him this afternoon," Shelley says.

The cat in question, Tang, is scratching at the screen door. Brenton opens it and picks him up. "You're a bad cat," he scolds him. "You mustn't get yourself killed. I don't think I could survive without you."

"You like that cat much more than any of us, don't you?" Shelley is looking at him curiously.

"He's much nicer to me than any of you," Brenton retorts.

As he sits down at the table, Tang still on his knee, Shelley asks, "What happened to the girl?"

"Which girl?" Brenton replies innocently through a mouthful of chips.

"You know who I mean, Brenton, the black kid that's been hanging around here."

"She's got a name, you know. You could use it. She's only been hanging around here for the last couple of weeks." He chews and swallows, and then can't help going on, "You wouldn't refer to Danny as *that white kid*, would you?"

Shelley clicks her tongue and gives an exaggerated sigh. "You're not accusing me of being racist, are you?"

"Oh nobody around here ever thinks they're racist. They're all as tolerant as anything in principle. But as soon as someone like Cal shows up everyone starts talking about Abos and black kids!"

"Drop it, Brenton!" Jason tells him.

"Where is she, anyway?" Shelley repeats her original question.

"She's in my room," Brenton replies.

"Well, I want her to go home and I'm going to tell her so!" Shelley jumps up from the table and storms down the **229** passageway. They hear the door to Brenton's room fly open, and Shelley start to speak. "Hey . . . er . . . Cal!"

Then her voice fades away. She calls sharply, "Brenton, come here!"

He pushes back his chair rapidly and hurries to his room. Shelley is standing with her hand on Cal's forehead, gazing in concern at the swollen foot.

"Brenton, she's really sick! Why on earth didn't you say so? That looks like blood poisoning! And her head is burning!" She is biting her lip, wondering what to do. "Where are her parents? We must get hold of them. Didn't you say she was staying at the caravan park? Jason could run over there while we go to the hospital. . . . Oh, hell, I promised Mum I wouldn't drive after dark and by the time we get back from Willstown it will be. Jason must take us all into Willstown and then go and find her parents."

"They aren't at the caravan park," Brenton tells her. "They've . . . they've gone away!"

"They can't have just left her on her own!"

"No, no, she ran away from them . . ." he improvises, but stops when he sees from her face that she is not believing a word. "Oh, Shell, I can't explain it to you. She's not what you think she is . . ."

"She's as ill as I think she is, if not worse," his sister responds. "And I think we should get her to the hospital right away."

"No!" he shouts back, making Cal stir and moan on the bed. "No, we can't take her to the hospital. You don't understand. She doesn't want to go. She doesn't want anyone to know who she is. I've got to get her home myself."

"Well, tell me where she lives," Shelley says, making a huge effort to sound reasonable, "and we'll drive her over
230 there."

"You can't drive her. I've got to take her. If I can get her down to the beach, then I think she'll be all right."

Shelley is gazing at her brother as if he has gone completely mad. "This is a very sick kid, and you're talking about taking her down to the beach?"

"She's not a kid, for a start. She's a very advanced and intelligent adult. She's an alien, for heaven's sake, and she wants to get home."

"Brenton," Shelley exclaims. "This isn't the time for your crazy games."

"It isn't a game!" he cries in frustration. "It's the truth. She's an alien. She's from another world. She brought the necklace . . ." His voice trails away at the utter disbelief on Shelley's face. "Ask Vicky," he continues urgently. "She knows it's true. She's the one who found her first. Vicky, tell her it's true."

Victoria is silent, not knowing what to say. Cal's life? Brenton's life? How can she choose between them? She says nothing, hoping the choice will be taken out of her hands.

"Don't involve Vicky," Shelley says sharply. "She's much too sensible to believe you."

"I do believe him!" Vicky cries, stung into words. "Only . . ."

"I'll show you!" Brenton shouts, and runs from the room, dashing through the kitchen, where Jason is sitting eating fish and chips on his own, and out to the shed.

"Jason!" Shelley calls. "Come here, will you?" When he arrives at the door she says urgently, "This kid is ill—do you think we should take her to the hospital?"

Jason also feels Cal's forehead, and whistles. "I reckon! You want me to drive you in?" He bends over and lifts Cal in his arms. "Gee, you're a featherweight," he tells her, as **231** she opens her eyes in alarm. "Don't be scared. We're going to get you somewhere where they'll make you better."

2 BRENTON is coming out of the shed with Cal's pack in his hands. Jason crosses the yard toward his car, Cal in his arms, floppy and disjointed like a plant that has started to wither.

"Look at this!" Brenton shouts. "This is what she brought with her. Look at how weird it is; you can't pretend this is anything earthly."

"Do you think we should take him to the hospital too?" Jason says over his shoulder to Shelley.

"Don't joke about it!" she replies sharply. "Suppose he's really going round the twist! What on earth am I going to do with him? I'm not taking him into Willstown with us if he's going to go on raving like this, and I can't leave him here on his own. We might be hours."

"Look at it, Shelley," Brenton continues insistently. "Use your eyes for once in your life. Look at the necklace too. You can't pretend they're ordinary." Then his face changes as he hears another car. "Oh, cripes, not that woman! What the heck does she want?"

The Toyota swerves to avoid the Valiant and comes to a halt alongside the group of young people.

"Heard your parents were away," Pam says through the window. "Just came up to make sure you were all right." In her quick, malicious way she has already taken in the scene and drawn her own conclusions. "What's the matter with the kid? She sick?"

Shelley's relief that an adult has appeared overrules her misgivings about Pam. "We don't know what's wrong with her. Her foot is terribly swollen and she's very hot. We were just going to take her over to the hospital."

"I told her she should have that foot seen to." Pam smiles almost in satisfaction. "I knew it was going to get crook. Hop in here, Jason, I'll run both of you in."

"No," Cal whispers in alarm.

"No!" Brenton shouts. "She doesn't want to go. And if she does go, I've got to go with her!"

"You're not going, Brenton," Shelley tells him firmly. "I think that's the best thing to do," she says to Pam and Jason. "If you two don't mind."

Jason is already getting awkwardly into the front of the pickup. Cal moans in his arms. Brenton screams, "You can't take her away. You can't steal her like that. You've got to let me come too!"

But the doors are shut and the vehicle is already in gear. He twists out of Shelley's arm, which is restraining him, and hurls himself at the side of the car.

"Brenton!" Shelley pleads with him. "Brenton, what on earth is happening to you?"

He has landed on his hands and knees in the dust. The Toyota is disappearing down the driveway. He runs futilely after it for a few meters and then slows to a halt, swearing furiously after them.

"How could you do that?" he demands, turning back to Shelley. "You sold me out, you betrayed me to her, you let her take Cal away to the hospital."

"Don't be so stupid, Brenton. She had to go to the hospital, she's really sick. And it's good that Pam came when she did. She's an adult; she can take charge; she knows what to do."

"Adults!" he says in despair. "Adults! Didn't you notice she was pleased Cal was sick. She was! Just like when I was caught in the net. She was pleased. She likes it when the worst happens, especially if it's something she's warned you about." Inwardly he is cursing himself for not being able to assume control of the situation, for being too small and too young to enforce upon the others what he knows to be right.

"She hasn't even got her pack with her," he says in despair, looking at it in his hand. "I've got to get this to her, at least. Shelley, can you please drive me in to the hospital?"

"No, I can't," she snaps back. "I promised Mum I wouldn't drive at night, and it'll be dark before we get back. I'll take you in the morning. You'll have to wait till then."

Something is happening inside Brenton's brain. It feels as though there is an electrode planted inside his brain and someone keeps switching on the current. For a few moments he is filled with terror as he wonders if he really is going mad, but then the impulses become decipherable, and he realizes it is Cal, calling for help.

"I'm going inside," Shelley tells him. "I think I could do with a drink!"

Brenton looks at her in disbelief. "Oh great! The answer to all life's problems. You're getting to be just like Dad. Anything goes wrong, have a drink!"

Victoria says in a small miserable voice, "Nobody's fed the animals. We'd better do that, hadn't we?"

3 THE ROUTINE's necessity, and the warm, living animals, bring some comfort to Victoria, but Brenton is silent and remote as he helps her. The kids jump and butt each other in play, bringing a smile into her eyes, but he acts as if he cannot see them.

"What are we going to do?" she finally ventures to ask him when they are locking the chicken sheds.

He gives her a suspicious look. It hurts her deeply. "I'm sorry I didn't say anything else!" she cries out. "But I don't know what else I could have said—or done. Shelley was never going to believe you—and then that woman turned up and took it all out of our hands."

Brenton considers her for a moment. Even though he feels as though she let him down and is therefore an unreliable ally, she is the only other person in the world who knows what he knows about Cal, and so she is the only person in the world he is the least bit interested in talking to.

"You won't go and tell anyone else? You won't tell Shelley?"

"I don't know!" Vicky bursts out. "It all depends on . . ."

"On what?"

"On if Cal's going to try and take you back with her!"

"Vicky, she's in no state to take anyone anywhere with her. She's calling out to me inside my head all the time. I'm afraid she's going to die! I've got to do something for her. I can't just let her stay all alone in a hospital. You know what things are like for her—she hates people touching her, and it'll all seem so primitive. It'll probably be like **235** torture. And if they try to give her any drugs they're just as likely to kill her as to make her better."

"Then we should go and tell someone who she really is," Victoria suggests.

"That's what I keep thinking. But she doesn't want that. And nobody ever believes what I say—have you noticed that? They've got it into their heads that I'm a bit of a nutter. And anyway, I don't know if it would be any better if they did believe me. It'd be just like in *E.T.*"

"I've never seen *E.T.*"

"They'd make her into some kind of specimen. It'd be awful." Brenton is thinking of Cal's physical frailty, her blackness, and seeing her subjected to expert scientific investigations. He heaves a deep sigh. "All I can think of is I've got to get over to the hospital. I've got to get her pack to her. That's the least I can do. I'll go as soon as everyone's asleep."

"How are you going to get there?"

"I'll walk if I have to, hitch a ride, whatever. As long as I can avoid that woman," he adds.

4

THE WOMAN herself is just dropping Jason back at the house when Brenton and Victoria cross the yard.

"They're keeping Cal in overnight," Jason tells them. "But they don't seem to be too worried about her. It's just an infection; it'll clear up as soon as they get some antibiotics into her."

Vicky shoots a glance at Brenton, who is biting his lip.

236 Neither of them says anything.

"I sure hope they can save that foot," Pam adds grimly. "It didn't look too good to me. And they need to know where her family is," she continues. "Where she's from. I said you'd go over tomorrow and tell them, otherwise they'll have to contact the police."

"Thanks for the lift," Jason says as she prepares to reverse.

"Glad to be able to help out," she replies. "Watch your step, kids."

"How is she?" Shelley inquires as she comes out of the house.

"She's going to be all right," Jason tells her, putting his arm around her.

"You see!" Shelley directs an *I told you so* look at Brenton. "You didn't have to throw such a fit. You happy now?"

"Sure," he replies untruthfully.

5 IT'S PITCH DARK when Brenton, clutching the pack, slides open the screen on his window and climbs stealthily out onto the veranda. From the southwest a huge mass of black cloud is swallowing up the stars one by one. By the time he gets to the end of the driveway, it is starting to rain, large drops like tears.

He's standing on the side of the road wondering how on earth he is going to get to Willstown when, through the rapidly increasing noise of the storm, he hears the sound of a car approaching, a very noisy one, without a muffler. Swiftly he runs across the road and starts waving.

The car rounds the bend, the driver spots him, and stops. As the window is wound down a voice Brenton has heard **237** before says, "Hey man, what the hell are you doing standing there in the rain? Hop in, I'll give you a ride to wherever it is you're going."

Wiping the rain from his eyes, Brenton sees, leaning across the front seat with dark face and flashing grin, the phantom graffiti artist.

"I was going to fix that new fence," he explains to Brenton, once they are on their noisy way to Willstown. "It's been bugging me for some time. It just needs a nice message on it. I had everything all lined up, all the gear in the car and, dammit, down comes the rain. You can't paint on a wet surface, and anyway I don't fancy getting pneumonia."

Brenton breathes out deeply and expressively. "I'm glad you came along when you did! I was wondering how I was going to get to Willstown."

"Long walk," the stranger agrees. He doesn't say anything else. He seems to think there is nothing unusual about wanting to get to Willstown in the middle of the night in the pouring rain. It's hard to talk anyway because of the drumming on the roof. The headlights reflect back off an almost solid wall of water. Inside the car it's like being in a little time capsule. The warmth and the passivity are making Brenton sleepy. His eyelids keep drooping shut, and once or twice his head gives a massive roll forward as though he's going to dive into sleep.

When they're a couple of miles out of Willstown, the phantom graffiti artist breaks the silence. "How d'you like my work?" he inquires.

"Your work?" Brenton comes awake with a start.

"Yeah, the pieces on the store and on the hospital wall. I consider myself an artist, you know. My whole life is a work of art, a dramatic presentation with lasting results. But
238 the nature of my medium is that I very rarely have an

audience, and I don't get much feedback, especially not out here in the sticks. In the city I sometimes take a train ride past my masterpieces and listen to what people say about them. What do you think of them?"

Brenton hesitates. "I don't know how to explain it, but they seem to mean something special—special to me, that is. They seem to be tied up with my life at the moment. It's a bit creepy. I've been wanting to ask you for ages what they really mean."

For a few moments the young man says nothing though Brenton has the feeling he is smiling. The rain pounds on the roof. The tires swish on the road. Then he speaks rather quietly, so Brenton has to strain to hear him. "Mean? I don't know that I can explain what they mean. I just stand there, facing the empty space, and the words come to me. They feel right, so I put them into the space. They can mean whatever you want them to mean."

"My father hates them."

"Wonderful!" the artist replies. "You've got to fight back, you know," he adds as they swing past the rotary and into Willstown. "You've got to do something. You've got to use whatever's at hand. And it's every man for himself. No one's going to help you." He shoots a glance at Brenton's tired face. "You seem to be a bit of a night prowler yourself. You can come out with me sometime if you like."

"It's funny you should say that! I've already got some cans!"

"No kidding! Too bad it's so wet, now. We could have nipped back and done that gross fence together."

"I've got something else I've got to do tonight," Brenton replies.

6 NO ONE has got around to repainting the hospital yet, and so the new building is still covered with the orange and green letters that spell out DEAD END DEAD END DEAD END. Brenton shivers when he sees it, afraid of what it may predict. The artist looks at it admiringly.

"Thanks," Brenton says as he climbs out of the car.

"No worries! See you later!" With a throaty roar the car accelerates, and the red taillights disappear in the rain.

7 THE FRONT entrance of the hospital is all locked up for the night. As Brenton runs around to Casualty through the rain he notices what the warmth and noise of the car prevented him noticing before. The insistent pulse in his brain has ceased. His mind goes out in search of Cal, questing like a dog, this way and that, but it encounters nothing but a vague blackness, from which it recoils in dread.

"No!" he cries aloud as he runs to the lighted doors of the hospital. "No!"

8 CASUALTY is deserted and silent, but down the corridor around the Intensive Care Unit there is a flurry of activity, the hurried desperation of people trying to save life. Brenton runs toward it, his fingers pulling helplessly at the impenetrable material of the pack.

"Wait, Cal, wait! I'm coming, I'm coming!"

But Dr. Greene is emerging from the room, his face frustrated and angry. Brenton runs to him.

"What are you doing here? You're Brenton Trethewan, aren't you?"

"I've got to see Cal, the girl they brought in earlier, the black girl."

"We've just lost her!" the doctor replies angrily. Then he seems to notice Brenton properly, the eyes bright with weariness and apprehension, the black hair plastered to the skull by rain. He repeats it more gently. "Brenton, I'm sorry. She's dead." He puts an arm around his shoulders. "We put her on an antibiotic drip for the infection in her foot, and she must have had a massive allergic reaction to it. That's the only explanation I can think of. It's like her whole system went haywire."

Brenton says nothing.

Dr. Greene goes on, "Perhaps you can tell me a little bit more about her. Was she a friend of yours?"

He nods, still not daring to speak, still holding the useless pack, twisting it in his fingers, unable to get at all the inconceivable power within it.

9 THEY ARE sitting in the nurses' station, and someone has put a cup of coffee in his hands. He is numbed by the realization that it is all over, that he will never see Cal alive again, never again feel the power and scope of her supple intelligence, never explore the realm of fantasy that she opened up to him, never again be recognized and accepted by her.

"The woman who brought her in said she'd been camping on the beach," Dr. Greene is saying. "You just met her there, did you? You don't know where she came from?"

He has come to the dead end after all; worse, it has turned out to be the dead end for Cal. She came from another time and place to die far from home, like so many other explorers and anthropologists—far from home among primitive people who killed her by trying to save her life.

He shakes his head. "No, I don't know where she came from. She was just someone we met on the beach and went around with for a little while." And that is all he ever tells anyone about her.

10 THE CEMETERY in Farborough is behind the town, overlooking the sea. Cal is buried here where pigeons and seagulls wheel and turn and cry above her head.

242   Only a handful of people attend the brief service: the

Uniting Church minister, the Trethewans and Dr. Greene. Afterward Brenton and Victoria drift away to the top of the cliff and look up the coast to Penbowie.

"Look," Brenton says. "You can see the caves." The memory of the night he crouched under all that rock looking for Cal's pack makes him shiver.

Victoria screws up her eyes. "I can't see them," she says in despair. "I think I should be wearing glasses." She puts her hand up to her neck where the necklace is now hanging again.

"Do you believe all that stuff?" Brenton demands abruptly.

"What stuff?" she replies absently. She is thinking about the necklace, the braingame and the pack, which she and Brenton have hidden away in case . . . in case of what they don't quite know.

"You know, about the resurrection and the life, what they say in the service."

"I don't know," she responds slowly. "Dad says it's like a hypothesis; it may not be an exact representation, but it's a handy thing to work with. It's a sort of model."

"You mean we never get to know the real truth?"

Victoria shakes her head. "How could we? There's too much of it to know."

There's another pause, and then he speaks again. "Where do you think Cal is now?"

"I suppose with God, whatever that means or wherever that is."

"And other clichés by Victoria Hare!"

Vicky looks down at the grass; it's silvery green, cut very short, and little yellow flowers like daisies are struggling to grow in it. "Dad says the universe is like a mind. Well, if it is, whose mind can it be but God's? And energy can't be destroyed, it can only be turned into something else. So **243** whatever made up Cal has gone back to being a different part of the mind."

Brenton is staring at her. It occurs to him that Victoria is as much of an alien as Cal. "Your father's quite a guy, isn't he!"

"I suppose he is. At least he's trying to be part of the solution, not part of the problem," she says, giving one of his favorite quotes.

"I wish my parents were. But then, if they were, you wouldn't be here!"

"I might still be in Africa," she replies wistfully.

"Do you wish you were?"

"Of course I do! But then, I've got to get an education. I can see that. Otherwise the things I'll want to do later will be pretty limited. Do you know something funny—a lot of Nigerian folktales end like this: *And they lived happily ever after and had lots of sons and daughters who grew up and helped raise the standard of education in their country.* Simon and I thought that was so funny when we first heard it . . . Simon couldn't stop laughing. But it makes sense, doesn't it?"

"But what does your dad think about . . . you know . . . about the arms race and all that?"

"He says you have to live *as if.*"

"*As if? As if* what?" Brenton is not sure that he wants to live *as if.* He would prefer to live unconditionally. But that is no longer possible.

"You just have to get on with life, do what you can. You can't just sit around on the beach and wait for it all to end. One of his favorite sayings is, 'Live as if you will die tomorrow. Garden as if you will live forever.' "

She is afraid Brenton will say something sarcastic again, but he doesn't. Instead he looks toward the horizon where

244

the sun is burning away the haze. The sea is calm and peaceful.

"He is a sort of gardener, isn't he, being a plant geneticist?"

"Yeah."

Since they have been standing on the cliff top Brenton has counted to one hundred several times. The bombs have not yet started to fall. He has a sudden strong sensation that he may be going to live to grow up after all.

"Perhaps that's what I'll be," he says. "A plant geneticist. Some kind of scientist; perhaps I'll be an anthropologist." He takes the dice out of his pocket and throws them. He throws them far out over the cliff.

The sudden action startles the pigeons into flight, and as they soar upward the dice vanish into the sea. Who knows, perhaps one day some other cosmic explorer will come across them and will treasure them as artifacts of an ancient civilization.